Nude
Hooray f

As the black-haired woman walked from the surf to her towel and lay on her stomach to dry off, old Roy strolled up to her, leaned down, and removed his glasses. We trailed after him to take in the action up close.

"Hello there," he said in this low, seductive voice he must have practiced in secret. It was enough to make me gag. "Now, my faithful companions here say they're gonna murder me for sayin' this to you, but I think you're a woman who can understand when I say I just wanna lay on top of you and see where it goes from there."

I felt like dying on the spot, and poor old Scott looked like he was in the middle of cardiac arrest, his hand clutching his heart and his face the color of dirty soapsuds. The black-haired woman turned over slowly and stared up at Roy. Then she removed her sunglasses. She was not Marilyn—and not only was she not Marilyn, the expression on her face was the expression of a girl who's just been surprised to find a huge cockroach in her bed.

"Get lost, pud," she said.

Roy gaped down at her. "Who the hell are you?"

"Who the hell are *you*, creep?"

Most Pocket Books are available at special quantity discounts for bulk purchases for sales promotions, premiums or fund raising. Special books or book excerpts can also be created to fit specific needs.

For details write the office of the Vice President of Special Markets, Pocket Books, 1230 Avenue of the Americas, New York, New York 10020.

CALENDAR GIRL

**A Novel by James Ellison
Based on the Screenplay
Written by Paul W. Shapiro**

POCKET BOOKS
New York   London   Toronto   Sydney   Tokyo   Singapore

The sale of this book without its cover is unauthorized. If you purchased this book without a cover, you should be aware that it was reported to the publisher as "unsold and destroyed." Neither the author nor the publisher has received payment for the sale of this "stripped book."

This book is a work of fiction. Names, characters, places and incidents are either products of the author's imagination or are used fictitiously. Any resemblance to actual events or locales or persons, living or dead, is entirely coincidental.

An *Original* Publication of POCKET BOOKS

POCKET BOOKS, a division of Simon & Schuster Inc.
1230 Avenue of the Americas, New York, NY 10020

Copyright © 1993 by Columbia Pictures Industries, Inc.
Cover art copyright © 1993 by Columbia Pictures Industries, Inc.

All rights reserved, including the right to reproduce
this book or portions thereof in any form whatsoever.
For information address Pocket Books, 1230 Avenue
of the Americas, New York, NY 10020

ISBN: 0-671-79866-9

First Pocket Books printing May 1993

10 9 8 7 6 5 4 3 2 1

POCKET and colophon are registered trademarks of
Simon & Schuster Inc.

Printed in the U.S.A.

For Debbra, Owen and Brett

Acknowledgments

I am particularly grateful to the Writers Room, Manhattan's urban version of the McDowell Colony, for providing me with both space and valued friendships during the writing of this and others works. I would also like to thank Esther Margolis, who has acted as agent, editor, adviser and friend.

"I reckon I got to light out for the territory ahead of the rest."

—Huck Finn

One

I guess eighteen is a time of looking back—at least I seem to do a lot of that these days. I've started college, my adulthood is about to begin, and yet I'm still a boy in many ways. I'm standing here in my dad's old work area; nothing has changed in here since he went off to fight in the Korean War. He was killed over there, but here in the garage he still lives. I look around—his tools are neatly arranged on a table. There's an old photograph, wedged into the frame of a small mirror, of him and me standing in front of the house. The picture was taken when I was six. Dad's in uniform. It was probably one of the last times we were together, because shortly after that he was shipped overseas. Even back then I looked like I had the weight of the world on my shoulders, though I remember being happy. I was always happy around my father. My best friends, Roy Darpinian and Scott Foreman, tell me I overanalyze life: I categorize everything; I read something into everything. Maybe so. But when I look at that photograph, everything is very simple—I see and feel love.

I walk over to Dad's old rolltop desk and open a large drawer. I begin removing objects from his past. Most of them are broken mechanical appliances, the result of repairs that were never made: parts from a flashlight, a broken key chain, a pair of binoculars in two sections, a strange homemade ear-lengthening device. Dad loved things, he loved people and life, and I believe that if he'd come back from the war he'd have fixed that flashlight, that key chain, those binoculars and finished a bunch of other half-done chores. He would also have done something more about putting *me* together.

The thing is, you get so damn dizzy growing up. It's a very tricky business. Every time you think you've figured out the answers, somebody comes along and changes the questions. The one that always gets me is, why are we made the way we are? That's the kind of question that drives old Roy nuts when I ask it, but I *mean* it. It always seemed to me grave errors were constantly being made in the arrangements of a boy's life. For instance, the location of his testicles—they're in perfect position for a dropkick.

I guess it's because my whole world's changing,

what with going away to college and all, but I seem to be living in the past a lot. I remember when I was in grammar school there was this big national Howdy Doody contest; it was that same year Dad went away—1950. There was a banner stretching across the gym that read ARE YOU HOWDY DOODY? In the gym were about a hundred Howdy Doody look-alikes all milling around, waiting for their chance to sit with the town photographer and have their picture snapped.

I was only six, and I didn't know all the big things that were happening that year. Jack Benny was still our most popular comedian. Joltin' Joe DiMaggio got his two thousandth hit. And thirty-four percent of the men called for the war in Korea were classified 4-F. Dad wasn't one of them. But for me, the world was dominated by this ear-lengthening piece I'm holding in my hand and that I guess Dad never had the heart to throw away.

I remember so clearly when he applied it to my head, trying to give me the true Howdy Doody look.

"Am I hurting you?" he asked.

I was in obvious pain, but I'd never let him know it—I was a boy dying to be a man. "Uh-uh," I said.

"Because if it hurts, I can stop."

"My ears aren't big enough yet."

"You know, the more I pull your ears, the shorter your legs'll get. Do you want to spend the rest of your life as a little boy with big ears?"

"I have to look like him," I remember saying with so much passion. "I just have to. I wanna look like Howdy forever."

Dad's smile was warm and full of wrinkles, even though he wasn't really old—maybe thirty-three. "Forever's a long time for just one hero."

Forever was my father's favorite word. He used it so often and with such naturalness it was as if he could tell you exactly how many days were in "forever," give or take a week.

My two best friends, Scott and Roy, were also in the contest. I'd known them forever, which is I guess my favorite word too, and as I watched Scott limp up to the photographer's table and get positioned, I remember feeling this big, hard lump in my throat. Scott was without a doubt *the* Howdy Doody. He didn't need makeup or a special haircut or false ears—he was the real thing. He also had a wooden leg—he was born with part of his leg missing—and I guess even back then I was aware enough to realize that somehow or other he deserved it more than I did. Jesus, was I jealous.

When Scott stepped down and limped away, Roy swaggered up and took his place. Even at the age of six, he looked more like a hardened criminal than a childhood icon. He was clearly a good example of a bad example—a four-and-a-half-foot rotten habit who, even in the first grade, knew more about naked women than naked women knew about themselves.

"Smile. Say 'Howdy Doody,'" the photographer said.

"Howdy Doody," said Roy out of the corner of his mouth. His participation in the contest didn't seem all that motivated.

As Roy stepped down, his place was taken by a very adorable six-year-old girl, also dressed as Howdy Doody. I can see Becky O'Brien now as though it was only minutes ago. As she smiled, her eyes made contact with Scott's. The two of them had this little romance going on. You could see it in the way they never took their eyes off each other.

In the end, some kid from a small town in New York won the contest. And I, like a million other hopefuls, was left to pout in the dust of Doodyville. Howdy Doody will always hold a special place in my life, but even for me, the freckles have faded. Freckles have a way of doing that. And even though that kid in New York walked off with the big prize, Roy and I decided that Scott was the Howdy Doody of the universe. Forever after he would officially be known as "the Dood" to his two best buddies if not to the rest of the world.

An old lawn chair, rusted and bent, is propped against Dad's worktable and, looking at it, I remember that last summer he was with us. We would sit in lawn chairs in the backyard. He was an avid newspaper reader and he would have his nose stuck in a paper while I sipped from a bottle of pop and waited for him to give a fact or an explanation or something. When he read the newspaper, he read every single word. If he missed something, he would stop and go back and read it again. And he was always encouraging me to ask him questions—anything, no matter how stupid or unimportant. If it made me think, it had value was the way he looked at it. Usually there was an answer to every question, and many times we would find it together.

I remember one conversation we had.

"Dad?"

"What is it, Ned?"

"Did Jesus really walk on water?"

"That's what it says in the Bible."

"Did he have to wait an hour after he ate lunch?"

"He didn't have lunch that day, son."

He would continue reading the paper and sometimes, without looking up, he would reach out and hold my hand. God, I loved him so much. If they could've made a bubble-gum card out of my father, he would've been an instant collector's item.

And then there's the memory of my father in his military uniform, tightly holding my hand at the train station as we said our goodbyes. Mom stood there trying to hold back tears, and I remember feeling kind of funny about that—maybe embarrassed and angry at the same time. This was my dad in his uniform and he was a hero.

He knelt down and embraced me. "Ned," he

said, "someone has to take care of your mother while I'm away. Will you do that for me?"

"Yes, sir," I said.

"And read the newspaper so you can catch me up on everything when I get back."

"Okay. I'll read it. I'll read it every day."

"Not just the funnies."

"No. Everything, just like you do."

I can still feel the embrace and smell the freshness of his uniform as he held me tighter. "Be a good man, Ned. That's all anyone can ever ask of you." I could feel his heart pounding against my chest.

And there's only one more memory of that six-year-old boy who became me and his dad. A priest stands at the foot of a grave as an American flag is draped over the casket. I stand with my mother in front of the casket. Other friends and family have gathered for the service. Among the mourners are Roy and his father, Becky and her parents and Scott and his family, his father looking like an adult version of Howdy Doody.

The priest said, "Paul Bleuer will be remembered as a hero who died in a war for his country. He was a gentle man. He was a family man. He will be sorely missed."

That afternoon seemed three afternoons long. My father was gone. We would never be together again. How could I ever become a man without him? Even then it was a question I asked myself, and I've continued to ask myself all these years.

People began leaving the grave site. I remained there with my mother, holding on to her hand for dear life. I stared at the casket and tears slowly inched their way down my face. It was the first and only time I cried. The priest said my father would be sorely missed.

Sorely missed wasn't the half of it.

Two

Six years later, when Roy and Scott and I were twelve, the whole thing about Marilyn started. On this particular summer day in 1956, in our hometown of Indian Springs, Nevada, I was buzzing around outside on my bike doing wheelies and stuff. I had a playing card taped to the frame of the rear wheel and it made motor sounds as it struck the spokes—*haroom, haroom, haroom*. I loved that sound.

Mom came out of the house and headed for the car in the driveway.

"Ned, I'm going to the supermarket to pick up some vegetables for dinner. I'll be back in less than an hour."

"Okay."

"Honey, don't get those pants dirty. I just washed them."

"Yeah, right, okay." I hopped off the bike and turned it upside down. One of the pedals was stuck. I headed for the garage for a screwdriver.

I opened the drawer of dad's old rolltop desk and handled the tools real carefully, like Dad might come home at any moment and find his stuff disturbed or something. But he never would be coming home. He was killed in Korea in 1953, and I'd never gotten over missing him. I wondered if I ever would.

While looking for the right screwdriver I found this old watch of dad's someone had stuck in the desk. The back plate was missing. I rummaged around and finally found the missing part. I pieced the watch together, wound it, and held it close to my ear. It didn't work—the time was frozen at 2:09. Morning or evening? What year? And what was Dad doing when it stopped? I thought of him—frozen in time, too. I remembered when he took me to my first ball game and the time when I was six and he took me to a Howdy Doody contest —but Scott had been a much more awesome Howdy Doody. Thinking of Dad, missing him like crazy as I went through his stuff, I took my Timex off my wrist and put it in the drawer where Dad's watch had been. I strapped his broken Hamilton on my wrist.

Then I noticed something stuck in the very bottom of his drawer. Slowly I pulled out this Marilyn Monroe nude calendar, "Golden Dreams."

My God, I thought. Dad? *My* dad? I caught myself not inhaling for the longest time, then took a big deep breath. I stared at "Golden Dreams," really caught up in it. I thought of Scott and Roy. I grabbed the calendar and raced out of the garage, forgetting all about my stuck bike pedal. I ran down the street to find my friends.

And that was the way it all started. "Golden Dreams" was about to change three young lives forever.

Three

I found Roy and Scott at the corner drugstore. Scott was slurping down a lemon ice cream sundae at the counter and old Roy was huddled at the magazine section pawing through the latest crime and Superman comic books. Roy wasn't exactly an intellectual giant. I wasn't either, to tell the truth, but I did crack a real book once in a while. The Tom Swift adventures were pretty terrific.

"Dood," I said, "Roy, hey, men, listen up. I been looking all over for you."

"What's up?" Scott said.

"Put down the magazines, Darpinian," I told Roy. "I want you guys to get your eyes ready for Ripley's Believe It or—"

"What kind of pea-brained—" Roy interrupted.

"Roy," I interrupted back, "this is for serious."

I held out the calendar and waved it in front of them like a magic wand. Scott's eyes practically popped out of his head. Even blasé old Roy was impressed. You could tell because he started blinking really fast like his eyes couldn't take in enough fast enough.

"Look at these bosoms," I said. "So round. So—so . . ."

"Round," Scott added.

"This is a guaranteed for-sure boner," said Roy.

"A miracle of shape and contour," Scott said, shaking his head in awe.

Marilyn Monroe was our first naked woman, and we stood there poring over her features like pouring syrup over a waffle—that kind of hunger. For the three of us, the American way of life had just added one item—there was baseball and apple pie, and now there was Marilyn Monroe.

That night Scott and Roy came to my house for a sleep-over. We sat around in our pajamas staring at Marilyn and trying to write her a fan letter.

Scott traced her form with a finger.

"Wow."

"What an angel," I said.

"What an ass," Roy said. "This is a broad with a future in front of her."

"She could be president," Scott said. *"I'd* vote for her."

"Come on, guys, let's finish this letter," I said. "I'm getting sleepy."

14

"Read back what we got so far," Roy said to Scott, giving him a playful shove on the chest.

Scott cleared his throat. "'Dear Miss Monroe,'" he said, reading from the notepaper.

I shook my head. "Say 'Dear Marilyn.' It sounds more personable."

"I think you mean personal," Scott said.

"Whatever."

Roy stretched out on the bed and stared at the ceiling. "How 'bout 'Dear Miss Atomic Blonde?' How does that grab ya?"

"Let's stick with Miss Monroe," Scott said. He continued to read. He had a nice reading voice— already changing, getting deep, with just a crack here and there. I tried to talk as deep as him, but I couldn't bring it off for more than a sentence or two, especially with girls around. "'We've seen all your movies,'" he read. "'We're your biggest fans.' That's it so far."

Roy closed his eyes as though deep in thought, though you never could tell with Roy. He said, "All right, let's see. How 'bout 'We're your biggest fans. You don't have any bigger fans in the whole world. We love you, and we especially love your big pointy tits. They're like missiles!'"

Scott groaned. "No. No way. Uh-uh."

"Roy, what's wrong with you?" I said. "We can't say that to her."

"Are you kiddin'? Ladies love to hear that stuff.

Because they got 'em they don't think about 'em as much as we do. We have to let 'em know."

"I'm not signing my name to anything like that," Scott said. "You're a slob, Darpinian."

"Yeah, and what are you, a man or a mouse?"

Scott and Roy both yelled "I'm a man!" at the same time, and Roy followed by yelling "Jinx," catching Scott cold. Roy was always catching him in a jinx. When you get jinxed by saying the exact same words as somebody else at the exact same time, you can't talk again until the spell is lifted. By this time the penalty for speaking was so rugged that old Scott never dared to break the rules.

"Look, Roy," I said, "we can't write she has tits like missiles. I mean, we can't write that."

"Well, what do *you* think's gonna grab her?"

"I don't know. I think we should sound like we have *some* brains. If anything, tell her we think she's . . . a handsome woman."

"Handsome?" Roy gaped at me, or sneered, or did both. "Are you nuts? Why don't we just tell her she's a man. Talk about using your brains."

Scott couldn't stand it. He broke the jinx, saying, "Darpinian, if you had a brain in your head it would die of lonesomeness."

Roy smacked Scott on the arm and then dived on top of him on the bed. The fight was on.

We argued till the early hours of the morning about what to say to Marilyn. We must have rewritten the letter a dozen times. Finally, Roy licked the stamp and sealed the envelope, and we went to sleep.

As we slept peacefully, a violent storm raged outside. Suddenly a strange thing happened—a supernatural thing, I guess you'd say—that woke us all up. A bolt of lightning came through the window without breaking the glass and bounced off the bed frame. That night claimed three pairs of boys' Fruit of the Looms and burned the edges of the "Golden Dreams" calendar—but left Marilyn's body untouched.

We never figured out how the lightning got into my bedroom without breaking the window. My father would have known.

To me it was kind of like a sign from God. Or maybe a message from Marilyn telling us we were all on our way to manhood—or as close to manhood as we could get without shaving.

About a week later I found a manila envelope waiting for me when I got home from baseball practice. I needed a little cheering up. I'd struck out twice and made a throwing error from center field and was feeling a little too much like old Charlie Brown on a bad day. Mail has always cheered me up, but never like *this* particular piece of mail did. I tore open the package, and there shining up at me was a single autographed picture of Marilyn Monroe.

I got on the phone to Roy and Scott, and they

came rushing over to the house as fast as they could pedal their bikes. First thing, we started arguing about who would keep the picture.

Roy grabbed it and said, "See what it says? 'To Roy, Scott, and Ned.' You notice whose name she put first? Doesn't that clue you guys in? She wants me to have the picture in my house."

"That's a bunch of baloney," I argued. "It should stay right here because this is where she sent it. If she didn't want me to have it, why would she send it here?"

"This was the only return address she had," Scott said.

"Bleuer," Roy yelled at me, "you don't know your ass from your elbow."

Scott said, "Well, I think I should get to keep it at my house because—because I like her the most. And that's why—I mean, the thing is, I need it for religious reasons."

We ended up writing out this formal agreement that we all had to sign. Before we signed it, I read it out loud.

"Okay, here's the plan. Number one: each of us gets to keep the picture at his house every third month and alternating one day every twelve years on leap year. Number two: a guy can keep it at his place over the Christmas holidays with special written permission from the other two. And number three: none of us will be able to take the picture out of town should he go on vacation. This pact is binding on all of us for as long as we all live." I turned over the paper. "On this side I've drawn up an alternate schedule if one of us dies."

I looked at my buddies. "Do we agree on this?"

Scott nodded. "Agreed."

"Yeah," said Roy.

The three of us clasped hands and stared at each other solemnly.

Four

So everything I've told you so far happened when we were still kids. The years passed, and we passed from grade to grade—even Roy. We grew taller, we started shaving. Once a week. Scott, who continued to be the spitting image of Howdy Doody, was going steady with Becky, a great girl who had no problem with his wooden leg. In June of '62 we graduated from high school.

Roy had taken to the beatnik look—jeans, T-shirt, twister shoes with taps, his hair in a ducktail, and a cigarette dangling from his mouth. But that look was about to change—everything for all of us was about to change. Roy was gung-ho to be a soldier. He had passed the army physical and was due in boot camp in two weeks. He had decided to join up for a typical Roy reason. "We're all going to hell anyway," he told us. "I might as well go out fighting."

In other words, we had grown up in those six years, and everything had changed but one thing. Our love for Marilyn—our passion for her—was as powerful as ever. Maybe even more powerful. And it grew to fever pitch when the June 22, 1962, issue of *Life* magazine hit the stands. Marilyn was on the cover! She had been working on a movie called *Something's Got to Give,* but she was fired two weeks after the photo shoot. The caption read: "Marilyn Monroe—a skinny dip you'll never see in the movies."

The three of us huddled together behind the open magazine, trying to be cool. We were in the waiting room of Dr. Jenks's office where Roy was waiting to get a shot. We had to talk in whispers because the doctor's nurse, Mrs. May, was a mean old biddy. There were two other people in the waiting room, an old man and a pregnant woman, and they both had their eyes glued on us.

There was this one photograph of Marilyn clutching the side of the pool with this terrifically innocent look on her face, her leg extended over the edge. I knew without the shadow of a doubt that she was the most beautiful, luscious, delicious, talented, sensitive, fun-loving, sexy lady on earth. I knew that I would die for her gladly. All she had to do was ask. I whispered to Scott and Roy that my boner was sure to be followed by a massive heart attack.

Roy said, "She ain't half bad, for a woman."

Scott moved a finger back and forth over her picture and said with wonder, "I'll bet her skin's as smooth as this page."

"You're all eyeballs, Dood," said Roy. "They're jumpin' out of your head."

"I guess she's just talent to you, right?" Scott said. "Talent and meat?"

"Just look at her eyes," Roy said. "Read her lips. You know what they're saying? 'I want you to canoe me. I want you to canoe me *now*.'"

"Let's have a little show of respect here," I whispered to Roy.

Scott said, "Darpinian, cigarettes are destroying your brain cells. You know that?"

"I'd really like these pictures for my collection," I said. "I wonder if Dr. Jenks would let me have this copy."

The words were no sooner out than Roy, with a look around to see if anyone was watching, stuffed the magazine up inside my sweatshirt. The old man glanced up then, but luckily a beat too late to take in the action. I was really pissed off at Roy for boosting the *Life,* but I forced a smile on my face for the old man's benefit.

Roy suddenly shouted, "Hey, how long does it take to get a shot of penicillin around here? You don't fool around with the clap."

"Jesus, Roy," I hissed in a whisper.

The pregnant woman, with a scared peek at us, changed seats to one as far away as she could get.

The old man shook his head, clasped his hands, and closed his eyes in an attitude of prayer. I hoped he was praying for old Roy, who could have used it.

"How come this didn't show up on your army physical?" Scott asked Roy.

"Simple, pimple. I paid Dick Chekian to lift a leg for me."

"You got to be kidding." Scott rolled his eyes up into his head, more Howdy Doody than ever. "I can't believe the army means this much to you."

Roy shot us one of his cocky grins from the side of his mouth—his Mr. Tough Guy smile—but his eyes were serious. "I ain't marriage material like you, Dood. And college sure ain't gonna happen. So you tell me—what's left?"

"How about a little honest employment?" I suggested, punching him on the arm for emphasis.

"How 'bout you shut up, Bleuer?"

"Your dad must be taking this pretty hard," Scott said. Old Dood was a sensitive guy, always thinking of other people's feelings.

"My old man doesn't give a shit," Roy said. "He won't even notice I'm gone."

"That's not true," I said. We called Roy's old man Tiger behind his back. He roared a lot, especially when he'd had a few, but underneath, he wasn't all that bad. I figured he was all roar and no more.

"He doesn't figure Asia is far enough away," Roy said. "They're gonna have to send me to Krypton to make my old man happy."

24

I hated it when he started talking that way. It made me nervous. Here I was, wanting a father more than anything, and Roy had a father and the whole thing was a royal pain for him. Go figure.

"You know, Roy," I said, "you should just try talking to him for once."

"You talk to him. Go drinkin' and whorin' with him. I got nothin' I want to talk to him about."

The nurse, fat and mean, waddled up to us. "Roy Darpinian?"

"That's me."

"The doctor will see you now."

Roy winked at us, showing the old bravado. You had to admire a guy who never quit trying to impress even his old friends. He held out his lighted cigarette to Scott. "Don't inhale, Dood. You might like it. I gotta see if Darlene was worth the fuss."

He followed the nurse into Dr. Jenks's office, and Scott and I sat in silence. He picked up a pamphlet on pregnancy and started leafing through it. Scott was one of those guys who would read the phone book or the cooking directions on a cereal box if nothing better was available. I snuck a look down the front of my sweatshirt. The stolen *Life* magazine was safely stuck to my sweaty skin. I wanted to return it to the table, but by now the old man's eyes were shooting bullets into us.

A moment later Roy's screams filled the waiting room. Scott and I looked at each other and broke up laughing.

* * *

We walked home, Roy bitching about the shot. "That Jenks, he's like Dr. Jekyll in that story. He's all smiles, but he's a monster when he sticks the needle in you."

"You mean Mr. Hyde," Scott said. "Dr. Jekyll was the good guy."

Roy shrugged. "Well, Jenks ain't," he said.

We were all tonguing ice-cream cones; Roy's was a triple decker. He scraped the taps on his shoes against the sidewalk, creating sparks. I kept my hand pressed against the *Life* magazine inside my sweatshirt in paranoic fear that it might fall out and instantly be spotted as stolen.

When we reached Scott's house, his girlfriend Becky was sitting on the front porch. She was a pretty brunette and just about as intelligent as old Scott. I'd been with her in homeroom practically since the first grade, and I'd made a point of sitting next to her and copying her answers whenever I could get away with it. She was generous and never covered her paper.

Scott offered her a taste of his cone.

"Yuck," she said.

"What? What's the matter?"

"Butterscotch," she said. "I loathe it." Now that was one thing about Becky. Not many girls, and definitely no boys, could get away with using a word like "loathe," but Becky had the charm to pull it off.

Scott had proposed to Becky during the third

orbit of Friendship 7. Why the third orbit? Don't ask me. But it took me and Roy completely by surprise. I mean, this was the Dood. He was still eating animal crackers and swilling down quarts of milk. And old Becky—it seemed like one minute when our backs were turned or something she went and turned into Doris Day. You know—adorable, smart, wholesome, and the bluest eyes you'll ever see. But even with all that going for her, Becky's best feature was her father. Mr. O'Brien ran the local movie house, which in Indian Springs was like owning the Holy Grail or something.

On July 31, the Dood would become Becky's husband. The Dood . . . a husband.

And old Roy . . . a soldier . . .

Impossible!

For the first time I could see my inseparable friends becoming separable, and it wasn't a good feeling. Fortunately, though, there was always Marilyn. Marilyn, our Golden Dream, never changed, and we had remained faithful to her through the years.

When I left Scott's house I ran home, kicking pebbles as I went, feeling this tremendous urge to get close to Marilyn, to feel her right inside my skin almost. In my bedroom, with the door shut, I took my Holy Bible out of a dresser drawer. As a kid, the Bible never really held much interest for me. It reminded me of long church services and the minister preaching up a storm while I pretty much tuned out. Also, the language was kind of antique and hard to follow. But my father always said you should never judge a book by its cover because what's in between the pages is where you learn the most.

It was one of the greater mysteries of the universe for me that Jesus Christ had been born exactly on Christmas Day. I mean, is that a coincidence or what? No one could ever explain that piece of great planning to me. It was because of this that I started looking in the Bible for answers. But then I found a better use for it. I removed the pages and filled the insides with pictures of Marilyn and articles about her, so what I had was a scrapbook protected by the leather cover. I took the pictures from *Life* and, smoothing out the corners, added them to my already extensive collection.

"You should never judge a book by its cover because what's in between the pages is where you learn the most." That's what my dad had told me before he went off to war, and that was certainly the case with my Bible. Fading leather on the outside, but inside . . . oh boy, inside, there was my secret life, my Golden Dream. My Marilyn . . .

Five

The three of us spent the next few days putting together more Marilyn *memorabilia*—a word I learned from Scott. It was like we all knew we'd soon be going our separate ways and it was important to get our Marilyn affairs in order.

Some Like It Hot came to the Coronet that Friday, and Scott, who worked there as an usher for Becky's old man, gave us a private screening. Old Dood jump-started the film in the projection booth, then ran down to join me and Roy in the center of the theater.

Three big shots, I thought. Young hot-shot producers having their own private screening at one in the morning. *News flash: Ned Bleuer, Scott Foreman, and Roy Darpinian, the hot new producing team, are hard at work planning Monroe's new starring vehicle.* Scott was chomping away on his chewing gum as he watched the screen, and Roy watched the movie through his 3-D glasses.

When it was over and while the credits rolled, Scott went back to the booth to rewind the film and I took over his job cleaning the aisles—popcorn containers and crap. Roy, naturally, just sat there watching me.

"Don't strain yourself, Darpinian."

Ignoring the comment, he lit up a cigarette. "I'm tellin' you, Ned, she's ripe for the pickin'. She ain't married to that Miller guy anymore. She just got canned from her new picture. Probably up for some action."

I reached under a seat for a candy box. Milk Duds—unopened! My lucky night! I shoved the box into my hip pocket.

"Don'tcha think?" Roy said.

"She's a very private person," I said. "You know that. We've read it in a million interviews."

"I'd like to meet her before I go get my balls shot off."

"There's no war on," I pointed out.

"Once I'm in, there will be. I just want to meet her once, Ned. That's all I'd need. *Boowang!* Boner heaven!"

"You'd never get in to see her. No way. But if you did get in, she wouldn't go out with you because you have no brains and you fart."

Scott limped into the auditorium and began helping me clean up.

"It can't be that tough," Roy said. "I'll just go up to her door and ring the bell. When she opens up, I'll say 'Put out or get out.'"

"That's sure to grab her," I said.

Scott looked up. "Grab who?"

"Darpinian's having a waking wet dream. He thinks Marilyn would go out on a date with him."

"You wish," Scott said.

"Listen, you guys, this is important. I'm goin' in the army, you're getting married, Dood, and Ned, you're off to college. We're breakin' up soon, and what've we done about Marilyn? Doodley-squat, that's about the size of it. It's a one-day drive to her place. We can hang out at my uncle Harvey's."

"I can't go with you," Scott said. "I wouldn't know how to tell Becky about this. And lying's out. We don't lie to each other."

Roy grinned, folded his lit cigarette into his mouth, then back out, an old trick of his that never failed to make me feel nauseated. "Snow her, Dood," he said. "Tell her you ain't ever gonna see me again and you want to spend some last minutes with your best friends just goofin' around. You got the face to sell it. You got the sincerity."

"I can't lie to her like that. She'd never forgive me. You want me to be a sincere liar?"

"Sure. Why not?"

"That's an oxymoron, Roy."

"A what-moron?" Roy shook his head in disgust. "Christ, Dood, you read too many books. You got no common sense or gumption."

"I'm engaged to be married. I take that seriously."

"You're a candy ass, is what you are. What about you, Bleuer?"

"I don't know," I said. "I'm not sure I could get the time off work."

"Then quit. Simple, pimple."

That was old Roy's solution for everything that became too big a problem. Having trouble in school? Cut class. Job getting to be a drag? Quit. Girlfriend pressing too much? Cheat on her. I loved Roy—I always would—but his values were for the birds.

"Roy," I said, trying to be humorous, "quitting requires an extreme knowledge of not working. I don't have your talent for free time."

"I'm talking about meeting her. *Her.* The queen of the universe. The woman you been dreamin' and creamin' about for years."

"You're not just talking about meeting her," I said. "You're saying you're gonna take her out. Are we all part of this hypothetical date? And what about money? Who's gonna pay for all this?"

Roy flipped his cigarette into the aisle and ground it out under his shoe.

Scott swept up the shreds with a disgusted mutter. "Maybe the army'll straighten you out, Darpinian," he said.

Roy stared at Scott, his eyes big and sorrowful. When he had that look, you thought of a homeless, undernourished kid. "You know the trouble with you guys? You really want to know? Neither of you have ever eighty-sixed this stinkin' little town. I'm the only one you know who's got the balls to bring this off. And if I do it and you don't, you know what's gonna happen? You're both gonna shrivel up and die. You'll eat your hearts out for the rest of your lives. Come on, men—four or five days of real livin'."

"That long?" Scott said.

"Whatever," Roy said with a shrug.

I sat at the kitchen table the next day eating a bowl of Frosty O's and watching an episode of "Clutch Cargo" on TV. There were three empty milk bottles standing on the table waiting to be collected, and I was working on a fourth, right from the bottle, to add to the collection. Roy's plan was buzzing around in my head; it had kept me awake half the night—unusual for me. I can usually sleep through an earthquake, in a manner of speaking, although we don't have earthquakes in Indian Springs. My attention wandered from the TV to my Bible, which was open to the photograph of Marilyn with her leg draped over the edge of the pool.

I heard Raymond, the milkman, clattering up the back steps with his case of milk bottles. The screen door opened with a squeak and Raymond stuck his head in the door.

"Anybody home?" he said, looking at me.

"Hi, Raymond."

"You know, it takes forty-three muscles to frown and only seventeen to smile. Smiling is less work." Raymond breezed in, a big smile filling his already full face. He scooped up the empties from the table and placed three fresh ones in the refrigerator.

"Thanks for the word," I said. "I'm not feeling too chipper this morning."

"Not much more to go, eh, Ned? What, a month, month and a half?"

"End of August."

"Your dad, God rest his soul, he must be grinning from ear to ear right now. Little Ned. Mr. College Boy."

I looked up at Raymond. He struck me as a smart guy. He seemed more thoughtful than most older guys in Indian Springs. "How come you never went to college?" I asked.

"Nobody in my family did. No money. And . . . I don't know, nobody expected it. You think I'd be delivering milk if I had an education?"

"I guess not," I said. "But my father went to Harvard and he ended up owning a toy store."

"Your dad wanted a family more than anything. It seems like before you were born, even before your mom came into the picture, that was all he ever talked about. And when you came along, *you* were all he ever talked about."

"Yeah, but how did he know the life he chose would be right?" I hated the drift of the conversation but didn't know how to close it off.

Raymond picked up a milk bottle and held it out toward me. "Take a good look at this. What do you see?"

"A bottle of milk."

"That's what I see, too." Raymond nodded. "Not your father, though. He saw an almost perfect food. He saw the cow; he saw the farmer, the milking process. He looked at this bottle and saw starving children being kept alive." Both of us stared at the bottle in silence for a moment.

"You know that smile business?" Raymond said. "Seventeen muscles and all? Your dad taught me that. Every Tuesday I'd come by, he always had some interesting new thing to say, nuggets of information I'd pass on, like I was a walking, talking brain." Raymond's smile exploded into a chuckle. "He taught a lot of people a lot of things with his degree, and he never even knew it."

Mom suddenly appeared in the kitchen. She walks so softly I don't always know she's there, which is sometimes a problem. I quickly placed the open Bible on the chair next to me, out of her view.

Marilyn was my secret world—mine and Roy's and Scott's. I loved Mom, but she was shut out of that world, like everyone else; we weren't about to share Marilyn with anybody.

On my way down to the toy store to open up, I thought about Roy's idea. I unlocked the front door and turned on the lights, activating two slot cars that started chasing each other endlessly around and around the race track. I watched them and thought of being on the road—from Indian Springs to Hollywood, from Nevada to California, from home to heaven. The more I thought of Roy's crazy plan, the less crazy it seemed. I was ready to go along with him, at least in my fantasies. But I knew I couldn't get away. Mom, my job at the toy store, getting ready for college—too many things stood in my way.

Six

About ten o'clock that morning Scott and Becky dropped by the store and asked me if I'd walk over to the Tuxedo Shoppe with them—spelled fancy with the extra *pe* and all. Scott looked like he was about to attend a hanging—his own. There weren't any customers, I'd already swept the store and stuff, so I locked up and went with them.

We walked in silence for a block or two, then Becky gave me a nudge and said, "Who do you like better, Doctor Kildare or Ben Casey?"

"They're both creeps."

"C'mon, Ned."

"Oh, I guess Doctor Kildare."

"I like Doctor Casey," she said.

"It figures."

"Why d'you say that?"

"He's this real good-looking guy, right?"

"He's plug ugly," Scott said.

"You're both jealous," Becky said. "He's got all that hair on his chest. It's very mature."

Scott shot her a withering look. "You think a hairy chest is mature? It's like he's a gorilla. He's a gorilla doctor."

"Yeah, Becky," I said, "a hairy ape with his arms dragging on the ground."

"You're just both so jealous."

Scott limped along, kicking a pebble with his good foot. It didn't take a genius to figure out they'd been in the middle of a discussion or two when they showed up at the store, and I guess they wanted me around as an audience or referee or something.

"I just don't get it," Scott said. "Why do I have to wear a tux? I'll bet Ben Casey wouldn't wear one."

Becky sighed. "Because all the guys are wearing tuxedos. Honey, just wait till you see how handsome you'll look."

"She's right, Dood," I said. "I'm going to wear a tux. Wouldn't be without one."

He shot me a pained you're-no-friend look. Then with a little smile—almost crafty, for Scott—he said, "I told Becky about Roy's idea."

I tried to hide my surprise. "Oh, right," I said casually.

He winked at me. "Visiting his cousin?"

"Right, yeah," I said, nodding vigorously. "His cousin."

"Bobby," Scott said.

"You three are such close friends," Becky said. "I think you should have this special time together. Roy's off to the army in a few days, and being with his cousin Bobby, I think it sounds like a great idea, you know?"

I could hardly hide my shock—Scott the liar.

Becky took my hand and squeezed it. "And you two guys won't be seeing much of each other once college starts."

"That's true," I said.

"I'm glad you understand, honey," Scott said with that preacherlike sincerity of his. "The only thing that bothers me is, it's summer. And . . . well, we're always together. And we'll be apart for a few days."

"Well, maybe it's time we tried it," Becky said. "It'll be good for us. Don't you think, Ned?"

I nodded my head with this very serious look. I couldn't get over what a terrific liar old Scott was. Maybe the honest ones were the best liars of all when they put their minds to it.

Scott tried on a tux jacket. The sleeves were about six inches too short. He had arms like an ape. The tailor marked the inseam for adjustments while old Becky went right on talking.

"We're gonna have the rest of our lives together,

honey," she said. "I can surely give up a few days of summer."

"You're the greatest," Scott said, extending his arm as the tailor wrote down a measurement.

But then Becky got this thoughtful look, the kind my mother gets that makes me want to change the subject even before I know what the subject is.

"But if you want me to tag along, I can talk to Daddy. I've never seen Hollywood."

I thought the poor sap would die on the spot. All the blood in his face went south.

"I don't think that's such a great idea," he said with a calmness I marveled at. I was seeing a new Scott. "I mean, we'll be hanging out with Roy's cousin and all. And probably his cousin Bobby's friends? You know, horsing around—boys' stuff."

"It's okay, sweetheart," she said. "I understand. I really do. You just go and have a wonderful time." She turned to me. "And you have a wonderful time, too—and take good care of my Scott."

"Don't I rate a 'sweetheart' too?" I said.

She rolled her eyes at me in pretend anger. "Now *really,* Ned Bleuer."

Over her shoulder Scott winked at me again.

Late that afternoon I met Roy down at a gym in an old warehouse, where Roy's old man was the boxing trainer and gym custodian. Mr. Darpinian was sparring with a local boy and using him like a punching bag, really nailing him when the kid's mind seemed to drift. Mr. Darpinian was pretty old—forty-two, forty-three—but he had plenty of ring savvy.

"Get inside my guard," he said, puffing a little. "Protect yourself. Good. Block with your right. Now jab. Jab. *Jab*. Son, you're leaving yourself wide open." He flicked a glove at the kid's jaw, and the poor geek reeled backwards. He was basically defenseless.

"Block! Block! Duck! Defense, *de*fense! You're not gonna avoid every blow. You wanna kill me, all that wild swingin'. Don't give in to the temptation."

The kid lost his cool even more. He let fly a series of wild blows that damaged the air and that was about all. Mr. Darpinian countered with a hard right hook, knocking the kid to the canvas.

As Roy's old man finished battering the boy, we walked up to ringside.

Mr. Darpinian helped the kid to his feet.

"Son, if you're not gonna defend yourself, don't ever step into my ring again."

He glanced over at me and Roy, nodded grimly, and started removing his gloves. You could have cut the tension between him and Roy with a knife.

"You sure beat up on him," Roy said sarcastically. "Feel better?"

"Kid's got guts," Mr. Darpinian said.

"Yeah, everybody's got guts. Look, I need the keys to the car. I'm gonna swing by Harvey's for a couple of days." Harvey was Mr. Darpinian's younger brother.

"You're going to see Harvey?"

"Yup. He invited me."

"He invited you? When did he invite you?"

"What's the diff? He invited me—and Ned here and Scott Foreman too. Right, Ned?"

"Right," I said, trying to look Mr. Darpinian straight in the eye.

"Do I get the keys or what?" Roy said, tapping his foot, jiggling coins in his pocket.

"What about reporting, Roy? You shouldn't be going anywhere this close to induction." Roy's old man seemed to be wrestling with words and feelings. I felt kind of sorry for him. He was mainly all roar. "You have to stay around here. There are things to do."

"What things?"

"Well, you need to collect your thoughts. Get ready for . . . you know, a whole new experience."

"I ask for keys, I get a lecture."

Roy turned away. He said to me, "Come on, Bleuer, we got things to do."

"Roy, don't you walk away from me." Mr. Darpinian was struggling for words. "You're not going to Harvey's. Do you hear me, Roy?"

Roy clapped a pair of Foster Grant sunglasses on his face, stuck a cigarette in his mouth, and shot out of the gym. I trotted along after him, feeling pretty lousy.

I guess Roy had to walk off his anger, because he practically jogged across town back to the toy store. I had to close up for the night, and I realized with a pang of something—guilt, I guess—that I'd only actually put in about three hours and hadn't rung up a single sale all day.

"Well, get the paddles, Bleuer," Roy said after a long stormy silence. "We're goin' on a canoe trip. It's Marilyn time."

"I still don't see how I can get away."

"The Dood's goin'," Roy pointed out.

"I know it. I was with him and Becky this morning."

"Gettin' fitted for his penguin suit."

"Yeah."

"He buried the Beck just like I told him. She practically opened the car door for him."

"Scott lied to her."

"So? He's comin' with us, that's the main thing."

"But I hate to think of him lying. He's a straight arrow. The flag's red, white, and blue. Certain things just are."

"He's beginning to understand how the world works." Roy cocked a cynical eye at me. "How about you?"

I shrugged. "I want to come along with you guys."

"So? What's the problem?"

"I can't leave the store now. I just can't."

"Why not?"

"It's the middle of the week, for one thing. There's nobody to come in for me. Mr. Beggie's sick."

"The place could close down for a month, nobody'd know the diff. Come on, Ned, what the hell's keepin' you here?"

"I just . . . It's just not possible now, is all."

Roy stared at me, looking more serious than usual. "I know what the problem is. It's your old man. His toy store."

"It's Mr. Beggie's store," I said, my voice rising. "Mom sold it to him. And I don't want to talk about it."

"It will always be your old man's store," Roy said softly. "To you it will. And he's up there somewhere strumming his harp with his eye on you." Roy turned to leave me at the toy store before I could think up a smart answer.

"Just remember, Bleuer, you can't rub Ben-Gay on a heartache. We'll see you when we get back. But just in case you change your excuse for a mind, we'll roll by for you at nine tomorrow morning."

At nine-thirty—miraculously punctual for Roy —he came by, honking his horn as he pulled up, Scott in the passenger seat. My eyes popped open wide. Roy was driving his old man's brand-new 1962 Ford Galaxie convertible. It was Mr. Darpinian's pride and joy, and I couldn't believe he'd let Roy take it any farther than the corner grocery store.

I grabbed my bag in one hand, my Marilyn Bible in the other, and raced down the steps to the car.

"Get in, man," Roy said. "Let's roll."

"Yeah, *yeah,*" I said, jumping in. I slapped Roy's hand and whacked Scott on the back.

Roy sped down the highway out of Indian Springs, the top down, "Walk on the Wild Side" by Jimmy Smith playing on the radio. We had our directions all right—west, to Marilyn, to our pot of golden dreams at the end of the rainbow.

I nudged Scott from the backseat.

"Are we actually doing this?" I said.

"We are actually doing it, young Ned."

"Wow!"

"Wow!" he said.

"Yee*oow!*" Roy yelled into the wind as he pressed down on the gas pedal.

After a few more "wows" and "yeeoows" we dissolved in giggles and a flurry of punches. The great Marilyn treasure hunt was under way.

Seven

We drove all day, and toward dusk we hit the outskirts of Los Angeles. We drove slowly through the city, our necks on a swivel, looking this way and that, taking it all in—the Chili Bowl, the Tea Pot, Knudsen's Dairy, the Tamale, the Big Donut, the Hollywood sign shining up there in the hills—all the cultural high spots. Sam Cooke was belting out "Having a Party" on the radio.

"Just don't forget," Roy said. "I do all the talkin'."

"No, leave the talking to me," I said.

Scott shook his head. "Sorry, fellas. *I* do all the talking."

"Hey, you guys need a hearing aid or somethin'?" Roy said. "I do all the talkin', period."

"If you're gonna do all the talking," Scott said,

"we might as well just turn around now and head home."

"I do all the talkin'," Roy said.

"Listen, Roy," I said, "if you do all the talking, we've got a problem. We're never gonna get past Mrs. MacDonald."

"Mrs. MacWho?"

"Mrs. MacDonald, dummy," Scott said.

"Marilyn's housekeeper," I added.

"I say we draw straws," Scott said.

Old Roy gave us the raspberry. "Draw 'em all day if you want to. I'm doin' all the talkin'."

We got lost trying to find Harvey's house and asked directions about thirty times, but finally we rolled up, taking the curb, brakes screeching. You could hear a lot of noise—music and laughter and stuff—going on inside. A party was in high gear.

Harvey greeted us at the door. He was two or three years younger than Mr. Darpinian—maybe thirty-nine—but he looked and acted a lot younger. He dressed younger, for one thing, like a hipster. A large white bandage covered his nose. He embraced Roy, who looked a little embarrassed, and ushered us inside.

Roy said, "I told the guys all the way here, I bet there's a party goin' on at Harvey's."

"This?" Harvey waved a hand in the dark and smoky room. "This isn't a party. This is two hundred people talking about themselves. Come on, boys, I wanna introduce you around."

We followed Harvey, squeezing past throngs of Hollywood types. I squinted real hard at a few who looked familiar. When people stared at me, I felt kind of like a star myself.

"I haven't seen you since you were . . . what? You were like this high," Harvey said to Roy. He held a hand at his knee.

"What are you talkin' about? You saw me two years ago at your old man's birthday party."

"Oh, yeah, you mean your grandpa."

"Same thing."

"Right, yeah." Harvey nodded but looked kind of puzzled. "Was I there?"

I was in a daze, and I couldn't keep my mouth closed. All the women were knockouts, there wasn't a lemon in the carload, and my eyes kept jumping from cleavage to cleavage hoping for a glimpse of the promised land. I noticed that the Dood's eyes were pretty busy too.

A pair of cute redheaded twins approached us and draped themselves over Harvey.

"Doubling your pleasure, Harv?" Roy asked him.

"Yeah, I met 'em on a commercial. Guys, meet Candi and Randi."

"Hi, boys," the twins said in unison.

"Oh, Harvey, we heard about the skiing accident," Candi said.

"Poor baby, will your nose be all right?" Randi cooed.

49

"Better than ever. I owe you two a private lesson."

The twins moved on, and Roy laughed. "Yeah right, Harv, a ski instructor. Really man, what's the story with the noisemaker? You run into a jealous husband?"

"I had a few feet snipped off."

"You're kidding." Roy turned to me and Scott. "Outta everybody in the family, Harvey's got this real blockbuster Armenian nose. You could land a plane up there. He could keep his cigar goin' in the shower."

"Okay, Roy, enough with the comedy." But Harvey wasn't angry and you could tell he really liked Roy. I was happy and relieved that old Roy had a relative someplace he could stand and who could stand him.

Roy laughed and said, "I mean is his nose big? Whaddaya think, Dood? You see how it came to the door before he did?"

He had old Harvey laughing too. "You know, it took me a while to figure it out—why hadn't I hit it big yet? I had the talent. But it was the wall-to-wall nose that was killing me." He touched the bandage. "You're looking at my future."

A waitress passed by, and Harvey grabbed her sleeve. "Andrea, I see three empty hands here. What are we going to do about this?"

A minute later Roy, Scott, and I were busy

sipping our very first martinis, complete with olives. We carried them out to Harvey's sun deck.

Harvey breathed deeply of the smog and waved his arm in an expansive gesture. "Have a look around you, boys. Is this a gorgeous view or what? Look out there. Hollywood . . . the stuff of dreams. Everything you could possibly want . . . and in *excess*. Food, money, women. Nightlife twenty-four hours a day. God took one look at this stretch of the West Coast and said, 'Let there be Hollywood.'"

We followed Harvey out to the backyard. There was a kidney-shaped swimming pool and, beyond it, a full-size, fully equipped, aboveground bomb shelter.

Harvey pointed at it—with faint distaste or nausea or something, it seemed to me. "This is where you sack out at night," he said.

"This is your guesthouse?" said Scott. He could hardly hide his disappointment. He was real finicky about dirt and beds and stuff like that.

"It's a bomb shelter," Harvey said as though we didn't know. "I hawk them on the side. If you're gonna buy one, you gotta see what it looks like."

"You really sell these?" Scott asked.

"Roy told me you were an actor," I said.

"He is," Roy said.

"Yeah, acting is my profession of choice, but every time I unload one of these darlings I'm saving lives—and paying for my nose job." He put a hand to his mouth like a megaphone and shouted, "Hey, Sylvia, Delphine, c'mere. I want you to meet some people."

"In a sec," a voice—a pretty voice—shouted back from the house.

Harvey slapped Roy on the back. "This place is yours as long as you need it."

Roy squirmed under his uncle's hand. He wasn't exactly cool about shows of affection. "Like I said on the phone, I'm figurin' two days. Three, tops. Do some romancin', take a canoe trip"—he winked at me and the Dood—"with Miss Monroe. I'm headed for basic training Sunday."

Harvey grinned at his nephew. "Marilyn Monroe, huh?"

"Why not?" Roy said. "Wouldn't you take her out if you could swing it?"

"I'd take out her laundry if I had the chance," Harvey said. "I'll be anxious to hear how you guys make out. Get me outta bed if you have to."

Sylvia, a terrific-looking blonde, and Delphine, one ravishing redhead, joined us then. They each took one of Harvey's arms. Delphine kissed him on the ear, and you could see that old Roy was impressed. And Scott's mouth was open wide enough to catch flies—*butter*flies. You had to hand it to Harvey—he really seemed to have some kind of a life going.

"Sorry, baby," Sylvia said to Harvey, nuzzling his cheek with her lips. "One of your friends was telling us this awful joke. What's a Mexican cartwheel?"

"Girls," said Harvey, ignoring the question, "this is my nephew Roy and his buddies. They're gonna spend a couple, three days with us."

Scott and I exchanged looks, the same word on both our minds—"us."

"Welcome to Hollywood, fellas," Delphine said in this low and sexy voice, a voice that came from movieland, not a place on the map.

"Thank you," I said, finally locating my voice. "My name's Ned Bleuer—Ned."

"Hi," said Scott. "I'm Scott . . . Foreman." He cleared his throat, turned beet red, and added, "Thank you for talking to me."

You could tell she found Scott cute. Most women did. They really warmed to his sincere and shambling manner, and once they learned about his wooden leg they couldn't get enough of him. He took a sip of his martini and managed not to grimace. I must say, even I was impressed.

Eight

I guess you could say the three of us had been waiting for the next day for the last six long years, since we were twelve and fell in love with Marilyn and the "Golden Dreams" calendar. We were up early and out of the bomb shelter without even a thought for breakfast.

We had no trouble finding 12305 Helena Drive, the address of our goddess. We'd memorized that address and plotted the route leading to it a hundred times. We were all decked out in our best threads. Roy wore his sunglasses—they definitely made him look Hollywood—and Scott was carrying a small bouquet and a box of candy. I had my Bible open to the page of Marilyn dipping her toes in the swimming pool, looking so great she made my teeth hurt.

When we pulled up to 12305 Helena Drive, Roy let the car idle and we stared at the house. For a minute we just took it in the way a religious person might stare at a sacred shrine, though to tell the truth, it wasn't that great to look at.

Roy broke the silence, saying, "Okay, remember, pea-brains, this is my show. I do all the talkin'. Let's make some history." He took a critical look at Scott and me. "Run a comb through your hair, Dood. Stir up the cooties in there."

A fence ringed the house. We walked up to it and entered through the gate. We weren't too thrilled to see a Beware of Dog sign posted just inside. Somehow that didn't seem like a Marilyn kind of thing to do, and the house itself didn't seem up to Marilyn's standards, as Scott was quick to point out.

But there we were, standing before the gates of ecstasy. Roy polished the knuckles of his right hand with the palm of his left and then knocked. I waited for Marilyn to answer the door dressed in sexy, flimsy lingerie with that sleepy, come-hither smile on her lips. But my fantasy went up in smoke when this man dressed in a ratty bathrobe flung the door open and glared at us. He was not exactly a vision of loveliness.

He looked from Roy to Scott to me.

"Yeah?" he said.

"Is Marilyn here?" Roy said, matching the guy's gruffness, which wasn't hard for Roy.

"You got the wrong house, buddy." Old ratty bathrobe started to close the door.

"Is this one-two-three-oh-five Helena Drive?" I asked. Roy shot me a dagger look for speaking.

"That's the address," the man said. "But there's no Marilyn here."

Roy took a step toward the man. "Look, chief, I don't know who you are, but just tell her we're the guys who wrote the letter six years ago. Tell her that. And say it took us all this time to make it out here, but, hey . . . it's us."

Ratty bathrobe was not impressed. "What are you, deaf or what? Read my lips: *there is no goddamn Marilyn here.* Now get the hell off my property."

Roy crossed his arms over his chest, clutching his biceps—his tough-guy pose. "Read *my* lips: we aren't leavin' until she comes out."

"Hey, Roy," I said, "easy." Then to the man I said, "Sir, please, I don't think we're putting this quite the right way. Let me rephrase it. May we please see Marilyn?"

"Please?" echoed Scott.

The man's eyes clouded as though a thought or something was passing over them. "You wanna see Marilyn? Is that it?" He looked at us slowly, one at a time. We nodded. "Yeah, I see." His voice was suddenly very quiet. "Okay, I'll get her. Don't move." With an unfriendly grin he closed the door.

"You see?" I said to Roy. "Maybe you should leave the talking to me."

I hardly had the words out of my mouth when the man opened the door wide, a Great Dane beside him, baring his teeth. The man yelled, "Kill, Marilyn. Kill them, girl!"

She growled and sprang, but we were already running for the fence, Scott moving slowly because of his wooden leg. Roy reached the gate first but fumbled trying to get it open, so he and I quickly high-jumped the fence. The dog got to Scott, though, and sank her teeth hard and deep into his leg—the wooden one. The dog let out a loud agonized howl and backed off, whimpering.

"What did you do to my dog, you son of a bitch?" the man screamed. Old Marilyn went slinking back to the house, her tail between her legs.

Scott limped up to us, a big grin on his face.

"You nailed her, Dood," Roy said.

"I was lucky she picked the right leg. Or the wrong leg." Scott's brow furrowed. "I hope she's all right."

Back in the car I examined the Bible, where I kept all our Marilyn notes. "This doesn't make sense," I muttered. "She's supposed to be here— since February. She moved here in February." Then I saw my mistake. The correct address was 12305 *Fifth* Helena Drive, not 12305 Helena Drive. Roy—and even Scott—made my life miserable for the next few minutes as we set off to find the right address.

Twenty minutes later we found it—a much prettier house, the kind of layout you'd expect Marilyn to live in, with hedges and flowers and stuff and a lot of rooms. We walked up a long pathway, and Roy rang the bell. Then, being the impatient type, he knocked, or banged, on the door as he continued to press the bell.

A middle-aged woman opened up and squinted at us. I knew it was Mrs. MacDonald, Marilyn's housekeeper. I'd seen a picture of her in a magazine that had interviewed her.

"Is Marilyn home?" Roy asked. Old Roy didn't believe in the formalities; he got right to the point.

She looked puzzled. "May I help you?"

"Yeah, we wanna talk to her."

"What is this in reference to?"

"In reference to it's like private."

Her puzzled expression was turning a little cool. "Do you have an appointment with Miss Monroe?"

I stepped forward. "No, we, uh—"

"Look," Roy interrupted, "just tell her Roy Darpinian, Ned Bleuer, and the Dood are here. She knows all about us. Okay?"

"Would you excuse me?" she said and closed the door in our faces, none too quietly.

"You sure got one smooth line, Roy," I said.

"I've got a million of 'em."

"Each one worse than the one before."

"Fuck you, Bleuer. She's in there right now putting on some clothes," said Roy.

"I don't think so," I said. "I don't think it's going to happen."

But Roy was caught up in his fantasy. "She's walking to the door right now; I can hear her. She's comin'. . . . Door, door, right now . . . *open.*"

But the door didn't open.

"Hey, don't call me the Dood around strangers," said Scott, giving Roy a shove. "It's okay for you and Ned—and Becky. But that's it."

Roy brushed him off and rapped very hard on the door. Mrs. MacDonald appeared again, looking less and less pleased with us.

Grinning at her, Roy said, "Look, I shoulda been straight with you. I'm here to pick her up for our date."

"I asked if you had an appointment."

"He means he's here to *ask* for a date," Scott said.

Shaking her head, looking a little like my eighth grade teacher when she caught me looking at photographs of nude women that were stuck inside my Greek mythology text, she again closed the door in our faces.

The three of us climbed back into the car. Roy sat behind the wheel with a lit cigarette hanging from his mouth. He was definitely not a happy camper.

"What time is it?" Scott asked.

I checked my watch. "Two-oh-nine."

"Are you ever gonna get that watch fixed, Ned?"

"No way. I like two-oh-nine. I'm comfortable with it. By the way"—I snuck a look at Roy—"if anyone's interested, according to my scorecard we've managed to piss off a caveman, a dog, and a housekeeper. Percentagewise, we suck."

Scott sighed. "It's not like the movies, is it?"

"You can say that again."

"What ain't like the movies?" asked Roy as he started the car. Brook Benton's voice filled the car, belting out "Revenge."

Scott said, "Remember in *There's No Business Like Show Business* when Hugh O'Brian is watching Mitzi Gaynor and he says, 'You know, I'm gonna marry that girl'? And then in the next scene they're married? If this was a movie, we'd be having tea with her now or something."

"You're right, Dood," I said.

"We'd be in her pants," Roy said.

"Not in any movie I ever saw," said Scott.

Roy started rolling away from the curb, got as far as the corner, and slammed on the brakes. "Hey, what the hell are we anyway, men or mice?" He threw the gear into reverse and backed up to the spot in front of 12305 Fifth Helena Drive. "We came here to do something, and no ball-bustin' biddy Hazel's gonna stop us."

And so there we were again, at the front door. Roy knocking and buzzing energetically, using both hands.

This time we faced a new Mrs. MacDonald. Her mouth was a thin snip of wire and there was fire in her eyes. "I'm giving you boys fair warning," she said. "Get moving. The police are on their way."

She started to close the door, but Roy held it open. "Please, miss, please. I shoulda told you the truth in the first place. I'm real sorry, but . . . well, you see, she's my mother. I didn't want to tell you at first because I didn't think you'd believe me. I mean, it's kind of weird. . . . You know. I mean, you can imagine. For eighteen years you're motherless and sad, crying into your pillow at night, and then you find out who your real mom is. And your brothers"—he threw us a contemptuous look—"they aren't really your brothers at all, just peabrains that sleep in the bed next to you. That's the God's truth." He grabbed my Marilyn Bible and clutched it to his chest. "And I'm willing to swear on this."

As old Roy finished this stupefying speech, we heard a police siren in the distance—the not-too-distant distance.

"Come on, Roy," said Scott. "Let's move it."

But Roy had me caught up in his craziness, and I said to Mrs. MacDonald, "We only want to be near her for a minute—you know, wish her a belated happy birthday? That's all. Then we're out of here."

The siren seemed to be growing louder.

Roy eyed the housekeeper, a battle of wills taking

place. She completely ignored me and my little speech as she eyeballed old Roy.

"Come on, let's split," I said as I half dragged him off the porch.

A moment after she closed the door, the siren stopped. A moment after that, she was standing at the big picture window staring out at us. She turned and said something to somebody we couldn't see—*Marilyn?*—then laughed.

"Well, I'll be screwed and tattooed," Roy said. "So round one goes to the old biddy. They got a security siren in there. But believe you me, she hasn't seen the last of us."

Nine

The next morning, nice and smoggy and hot, muscle beach idiot weather, we were out in Harvey's backyard beside the pool. I was busy trying to get Marilyn's phone number from Information, Roy's new Zenith radio was blasting out Ray Charles singing "I Can't Stop Loving You" while old Roy was flipping through my Marilyn Bible, Scott was doing a bongo beat on his wooden leg, and Harvey was dancing around exhibiting the model bomb shelter to two potential buyers. Busy, busy—and boy, was I pissed! I wasn't getting to first base with the phone company, and I don't like people—even close friends like Roy and Scott—fiddling around with my Bible. It's sacred property.

"My best salesmen are Kennedy and Khrushchev," Harvey was saying to his two suckers. "Khrushchev sells one of these every time he opens his mouth."

I tried to tune him out. "Yes—Marilyn Monroe," I said for about the skadillionth time. "M-o-n-r-o-e. I mean, could you just do me a favor and tell me if she's listed or unlisted? The last two operators just hung up on me. I mean I'm a taxpayer and all. The thing is, ma'am, she *may* be listed, but nobody bothers checking because they assume she isn't." The operator, in a not very friendly voice, told me to hang on, which was progress. At least she didn't bang the receiver in my ear.

I noticed the ash from Roy's cigar—he was making deep inroads into Harvey's supply—was about to fall into the pool. "Hey, Roy! Hey, slob, watch your stupid stogie."

He responded by tapping the ash right into the water.

"Why do you smoke those things, anyway?" Scott said, wrinkling his nose.

"They remind me I'm alive. They make me strong."

"They sure make you smell strong," I said. "An old guy once told me every coffin nail you smoke takes fourteen seconds off your life."

"Maybe with your lungs," Roy said. "Not mine."

The operator came back on and said there were no listings; there were two unlisted phones. I knew one of those was white because I'd seen a picture of it in a magazine. So not being able to call her up and break the ice with a friendly little chat was one more strike against us.

Harvey moved his two suckers up close to the bomb shelter. "Radioactive particles are bombarding your neighborhood," he said in his sincere salesman's voice. "You want something that's gonna last. Like I always say, 'He who lasts, laughs.'" He waved the two of them into the bomb shelter and followed after them.

Roy's nose was deep in my Bible. Suddenly he looked up and let out a shrill whistle between his teeth. I always admired that damn whistle of his and could never get the hang of it. "Hey, Bleuer, did you read this? 'Her derriere looked like two puppies under a silk sheet.' That's choice stuff, man."

"Don't drool on my Bible, Darpinian."

"Listen," Scott said. "I hate to bring it up and all, but are we heading home tomorrow?"

"No, we are *not* headin' home," Roy said. "Tomorrow's a whole new ball game."

Scott shook his head and looked kind of hangdog. "We're never gonna get past her housekeeper. I say let's just call it quits."

"Dood, you can't rub Ben-Gay on a heartache. How many times I gotta tell you?"

"What does that mean exactly?"

"It means I don't rest until she's mine. It means

if you don't try, you got no guts and you end up hating yourself."

I said, "Roy, come on now, truthfully. This idea of canoeing her, it's just talk, right? I mean, Marilyn's an institution. You don't have sex with an institution."

"Wrong, Neddy boy. After she's been with me, I want her to say I'm the greatest lover she's ever had. Better yet, I want it in writing. I'll need proof in the trenches."

"Darpinian, you're a classic pimple," I said. "Get the Clearasil, Dood, the big tube, and send him to his room."

Right about then Harvey and his two suckers emerged from the bomb shelter, and old Harvey was still talking a mile a minute. "Bottom line here, a complete money-back guarantee. When the first bomb drops in *your* backyard and everything around you turns to rubble, if this fallout shelter doesn't work to your complete satisfaction, I'll return every red cent you put into it. No questions asked. How can you lose on a deal like that?" He gave them such a wide and dazzling grin, the Band-Aid shifted a little on his nose.

Scott, who'd rolled his pants up, suddenly began picking at an object protruding from his wooden leg. With a twisting motion of his thumb, like working a corkscrew, he removed something from his leg, brought it up close to his eyes and studied it.

"Jesus, you guys, get a load of this."

"A tooth," I said.

"That dog's tooth," said Roy. We stared at the tooth and then at Scott. Then Roy began howling like an injured dog, drawing a wrathful look from Harvey, and Scott and I cracked up.

That afternoon we tooled around Hollywood in the Galaxie, with my Marilyn Bible guiding us. With its help we went to see all the places she'd hung out in at one time or another—Jax Women's Clothing Store, Max Factor, the Roosevelt Hotel, a Mexican antique store, the City National Bank of Beverly Hills, La Scala restaurant. Even a church in Brentwood she'd attended. One of our stops was Schwaab's coffee shop. Scott hung his head out the window and yelled, "Hey, Roy, stop the car."

Roy hit the brakes. Through Schwaab's window we could see a blonde sitting at the counter.

"It's her," Scott said softly, in wonder. "She's . . . sitting right there. Oh, God, my heart."

"What makes you so sure?" I said.

"A blind guy would know it was her. I'm telling you it's Marilyn."

Roy didn't seem too excited.

"Whaddaya think?" I asked him.

"I think the Dood's an idiot. What's a star like Marilyn doin' sittin' at a counter?"

"Park the car," I said.

Roy shrugged, rolled up against the curb; we jumped out and tore into Schwaab's.

"Marilyn," I said, moving toward her. But when she looked up, she not only was not Marilyn, she wasn't even pretty. She stared at us like we'd just escaped from a funny farm.

I looked at Scott and Roy and said, "A graceful exit, boys. That's the least we can do."

"You're both idiots," Roy grumbled.

With no better plan in mind at the moment, we drove back out to Marilyn's house. We parked halfway down the block, where we could follow the action at her house without being seen. We had the top down and the radio on, and while we waited we played Ghosts. It was this great game we played when we had time to kill. The object was *not* to spell out a word of four letters or more; if the word ended on you, you'd get a fourth. Four fourths and you were a ghost and out of the game.

Roy started. *"F,"* he said.

"F-u," I said.

"F-u-c," Scott said.

Roy thought for a moment, frowned, scratched his head and finally said, "Shit, I quit."

The thing is, Roy frequently quit, and he was almost always the ghost. His vocabulary simply didn't include words like "fuchsia" or "fucose." But for some weird reason he liked to start with the letter *"f."*

"Well," he said, "since we're out here for the long haul, let's turn on some heat." He opened the glove compartment and pulled out a small package wrapped in tinfoil. He carefully undid it to reveal several neatly packed reefers. He handed one to Scott and one to me and kept the biggest one—the size of a cigar—for himself.

Scott looked at the reefer with disbelief and then at Roy. "What the hell," he said. *"Reefers?"*

"Hey, can't you make it a little louder, Dood? I don't think they heard you at the police station."

"Are these standard equipment on all 'sixty-twos?" I said. "Open the glove compartment and —bingo!—there's your set of reefers, compliments of General Motors."

"I borrowed these from Harvey."

"Borrowed?" I rolled my eyes at Scott.

"We're gonna go to jail," he said. "I know it. I can feel it in my bones."

"You only got one bone, Dood," I said. "And it's too small to have any feelings."

"I did this for you guys, okay?" said Roy. "The stuff'll put hair on you in all the right places."

"I'm fairly sure I have the correct number of hairs in all the right places," I said. "Thanks anyway."

Roy banged the dashboard. "You dismal chickenshits. One time, *just one time,* do something. Remember the Darpinian rule: how long you live has nothin' to do with how long you're gonna be dead for."

Scott and I looked at each other and then at Roy, knowing he was right. The thing about Roy was, just when you were convinced he was stupid he turned brilliant on you.

He lit the three joints with his Zippo. "See you this side of heaven," he said. Scott and I took small beginner's puffs on our joints; Roy inhaled deeply and held the smoke in, it seemed like forever. It took a second forever for him to exhale, and when he did he said. "That's the right way to do it, team."

We learned fast, and before our joints were smoked halfway down we were very, very stoned. Stoned and mellow. We talked and giggled a little and then lapsed into our own inner selves.

Scott, his eyes closed, said, "Did you guys ever think if Mr. Ed could talk, how come he never complained about standing in his own piss?"

"Profound," I said, hearing his words from far off. They chimed like a set of pretty bells. "Profound, Dood."

"You know the only reason I was born?" Roy said after another long silence.

"'Cause the drugstore was closed on Sunday," I said.

"I was supposed to be a girl. To make up for my sister."

Scott opened his eyes. "You have a sister?"

"She died. She . . . I don't know what was wrong with her. She died in her first year." Roy took a deep drag on his joint and hours later, it seemed like, continued. "My mom . . . well, let me tell you, when you're on top you're the greatest in her eyes. She'll kill for you. And the better you get, the higher you rise. Man, she digs a winner. But if your luck ain't runnin' so good"—he shrugged—"it's good-bye, Charlie. My old man, in his heyday, she just— He was king in her eyes. He used to get up for a fight by canoein' her. I could hear them goin' at it through my bedroom wall. Then he got busted up by this young guy on his way up. She just, she didn't respect him no more. Just like that. He was down, and it was fuck you. She didn't let him up. So he started hittin' the bottle and she just couldn't take it." A long silence, another deep drag, and Roy said, "She left us. She's a singer now, you know."

"I didn't know she was a singer," I said.

"That's a pretty sad story," said Scott.

Roy looked away and didn't say anything.

"This stuff is fan*tas*tic," I said, hoping to brighten the mood. I didn't want the sadness I felt to suddenly weigh me down; I didn't want to think about my father. "This— Listen. . . . I can hear my skin against my clothes. Can you hear it? Listen . . ."

"God, Becky's gonna go bananas," Scott said.

Roy gave him a push. "You candy ass."

"I'm double-crossing her."

"How do you figure that?" I said.

"You know, with Marilyn."

"Come on, Dood. We haven't even *met* Marilyn. We met her fence. We met her door. We met her housekeeper. We met rejection is what we met."

Scott was beginning to look all teary-eyed. "I'm a fink. I'm a rat fink."

"Dood, the only thing you've done wrong so far is gettin' a boner with somebody else's name on it." Roy gave Scott a soft, affectionate noogie on the arm.

"Ouch," Scott said.

"We're just out here to say hello, Dood," I said.

"I still feel rotten. Becky loves me so much. Why?"

"It's the phony leg," Roy said. "She's a sucker for firewood."

"Will she still love me this much when I'm old and ugly?"

"You're ugly now, Foreman."

"That's the beauty of it, Dood," I said. "Her love isn't based on externals. If it was, she'd scream every time she looked at you."

I guess the reefers wound us down to a halt, and we drifted off to sleep. The next thing I knew, it was morning. I rubbed my eyes and wondered if the foul taste in my mouth was from the reefer. Roy was sound asleep in the front with his feet up over the top of the seat. I looked around for Scott. He was seated motionless on a tree swing across the street. I got out of the car, cramps stabbing at me, and hobbled over to him.

"Push me," he said.

"Dood, eighteen-year-olds do not push other eighteen-year-olds on swings. Unless you're an eighteen-year-old girl, and then only if you're wearing a skirt and no underpants."

"Come on, Ned. Just for a minute. I've never—I've never done this before."

"You've been on a swing. What about all those times we went to the park?"

"I never went to the park with you."

"What're you talking about? We all went."

"Not me. You went with Roy. Just Roy."

I suddenly realized Scott was right. We'd done everything else together—hanging out at our houses, going to movies and stuff—but never the park.

"You know, you're right, Dood. I'm sorry. You could've come with us. I mean you could've come."

"I'm not a lot of laughs, in case you haven't noticed."

Because Scott was such a good friend I knew what I had to say, but it wasn't easy to say. "Dood, you gotta know by now, Roy and I don't think any less of you because there's less of you. You understand?"

We looked at each other, and then both of us looked away.

"So give me a push," he said.

I began pushing him, and the smile on his face was like the smile of a child who thinks he's going to be pushed all the way up to heaven.

"Higher, higher, Ned."

Roy walked up, yawning, and joined me in pushing Scott.

"Round the horn, Dood," Roy said.

He and I took a running start and gave Scott a hard push.

"Hey, look," Scott said, pointing toward Marilyn's house.

We watched as a green Dodge with Mrs. MacDonald at the wheel pulled out of the driveway. There was a passenger in the backseat we couldn't make out.

Roy grabbed the swing chains and brought Scott to a quick stop. "Guys, let's put some tires on the road."

"You think it's Marilyn in the back?" I said.

"Who else?"

We hopped in the Galaxie, which I noticed was starting to show its age real fast, and tailed the Dodge through a maze of side streets. We almost lost Mrs. MacDonald twice—for sure she didn't drive like an old lady—but Roy solved that problem by running a couple of red lights to keep pace. After about a ten-minute chase—Mrs. MacDonald had sped up and kept looking through her rearview mirror; she knew who we were—she made a sharp right turn onto a highway entrance ramp. There was only room for one car on the ramp but Roy hit the accelerator and tried to squeeze alongside the Dodge.

Jesus Christ, Roy," moaned Scott. "Take it easy!"

"We have a little car accident," Roy said, "nothing serious, and we get her to come out and swap insurance info. Right? Then I beg her for a date."

"You're insane, Darpinian," I said. *"Slow down."*

Roy finally gave way and pulled in behind the Dodge. "You are a mouse, Bleuer."

"Look, why would she possibly want to go out with a guy who just rear-ended her? Use your brains."

"They did it in *The Misfits*. Remember in the beginning guys kept crashin' her car so they could talk to her?"

"That's the movies," Scott said. "It doesn't happen in real life."

"A mild case of crinkled fenders would put us in contact." He gunned his engine a little, tailgating the Dodge.

"Roy, we are not going to have a car accident with her!" I shouted. "Why can't we just ease up next to her and roll down our windows?"

"I repeat, you're a mouse."

"Better a live mouse than a dead jerk."

"Bleuer, your old man's gotta be turnin' over in his grave just about now."

"My father? What about my father?"

"He's got a box seat for this day in your life. You figure he likes watchin' his son act like a pussy?"

"I know for a fact my father never got into a car accident for a date."

"Let's just go back and wait outside her house," Scott said. "Or better yet, let's head back to Indian Springs."

Roy said, "Let's head back to Indian Springs" at the same time as Scott and yelled, "Jinx!" at him. He reached over and punched Scott hard on the shoulder.

Suddenly the Dodge shot forward, passed another car, changed lanes, and disappeared from sight.

"Do you believe this?" Roy said. "The old lady's seen too many movies."

"Marilyn must hate us," I said. "She's gotta hate us. *I* hate us."

"Nobody hates nobody," Roy said. "It's the chase. They love it."

"How do you figure that?"

Roy hit the floorboard, weaving in and out of traffic, searching for the Dodge. "The old bag's givin' us the slip, for crissake."

"Jesus, slow down," I said. "Come on, man. You'll get us killed."

"Walkin', talkin' Jesus," he said. "It's outta my hands."

"Whaddaya mean it's out of your hands? Are you crazy?"

Scott's eyes were shut tight in an attitude of prayer.

Roy hit 80, 85, nearly 90 and ended up speeding right past the Dodge. I didn't want to say anything for fear he'd slam on the brakes. I could tell that Scott had spotted the Dodge too, but he could only whimper. He wasn't allowed to talk because of the Jinx.

"What is it, Dood?" said Roy. "Oh, yeah, I forgot. Unjinx. What is it?"

"We just passed her," Scott said.

"Sheee-*it!*" Roy slammed on the brakes just as I'd feared he would, veering to his right and rear-ending a garbage truck that was piddling along in the slow lane. We had to stop and get out to inspect the damage, immediately backing up the traffic behind us. The truck was fine, but Mr. Darpinian's car had a bent front fender. Roy didn't seem all that concerned; his eye was on the cars passing in the other lanes. Then the green Dodge appeared, in the lane right next to us. A woman stared out the rear window. She was wearing a head scarf, but she couldn't disguise her radiant, incredible, beautiful face. It was Marilyn! She looked directly at us and then an instant later she was gone. But it was an instant that we knew would live in our memories— mine and Roy's and Scott's—for as long as we lived.

Ten

Before going back to Harvey's place we bought out a supermarket and took six bags of groceries with us. We were famished, the result of no dinner the night before, reefers in the night, and no breakfast. I ripped open a package of Kraft Fudgies and the pick-a-pack of small boxes of breakfast cereals and began alternating between a chunk of fudgies and a mouthful of cereal.

Scott dug into a box of Oreos. To wash them down, he worked seriously at draining a six-pack of Diet-Rite cola. He pulled back the tab on the can, lifted it off, smiling as if he'd just mastered some new technique. Pop tabs were still pretty new in '62.

Roy stuck a fork deep into a pint of Sealtest

Neapolitan ice cream. As he struggled to pull out a forkful, he ended up pulling the entire pint out. It didn't faze old Roy one bit; he just took a humongous bite out of the rectangle of ice cream at the end of his fork. No problem.

"So we fired a couple of blanks," he said. "We live to fight another day. Just remember—you can't rub Ben-Gay on a heartache."

"Your old man's gonna kill you when he sees the car," Scott said.

"Don't sweat it, Dood."

"You made an instantaneous decision to have a car accident," I said. "It's like there's no editing process between your brain and your actions."

"Yeah, well, I ain't like you, Bleuer."

"You can say that again."

"You figure everything to death. You sit and think and don't do nothin'. Look at that book you lug everywheres. Sometimes you just gotta floor it."

"Appropriate phraseology, given our recent experience on the highway."

"'Appropriate phraseology,'" Roy said, mimicking me. "Just say, 'Screw you, Roy,' why don't ya? That's really what you mean."

I took a sip from a quart can of Stokely's Pi-Li pineapple-lime juice and winked at Scott. "I think I got Darpinian's goat," I said.

"My ass," Roy said.

"He *is* a goat," said Scott who was busy removing the pop tops from each and every can of every six-pack we'd bought. He had no intention of drinking anything but simply enjoyed the act of popping tops. "We don't even know why we're here anymore," he said, avoiding Roy's eyes.

"Don't start that shit again, Foreman. You're beginning to get on my nerves."

"The Dood's right, Roy," I said. "This is turning into pure stupidity. We're starting to irritate her. I don't want Marilyn to remember me like this."

There was a long, angry silence—solid enough to eat with knife and fork—while Roy gobbled some Nestlé's chocolates. He dived into a grocery bag for more food, fished out a strip of S&H Green Stamps, which he tossed into the sink.

"I'll tell you how we're gonna get into her house," he said finally. "We got to do something really special. We got to move her. That's it! Make her cry. She's a soft touch; you know that. She's all sentimental mush inside. She cries and she's ours. You guys got any ideas?"

"I remember this story I read once," I said, "but I don't know. It's really a stretch."

"Hey, anything can make a plan. Just let me hear it."

I opened my Marilyn Bible and turned to an article I'd only read a few million times. "'She has a profound empathy for animals,'" I read, "'based on her own memories of being unprotected as a child. Once, when it was raining, she heard a cow mooing just outside the door.'" I shook my head in disgust. "This is insane, guys. There's nothing here."

"No, no, no," Roy said. "Keep going. You're on to something."

"Sounds interesting to me," said Scott. "I can see Becky getting all blubbery over a cow."

So I went on reading: "'She tried to bring the calf inside the door, because she thought the farmer had forgotten it and left it outside to get soaked!'"

Roy leaned back, his hands behind his head, grinning. "This is the jackpot, men. The absolute friggin' jackpot."

"'It took Jim,'" I continued, "'who was her husband at the time, over an hour to convince Norma Jean that cows didn't mind standing out in the rain.'"

"Oh, but they do," Roy said, with this broad, comical wink. "They hate it."

"How do *you* know?" I said. "You're no farmer."

"I tell you this is it. We've got our visa to Marilyn."

Scott nudged me. "The Darpinian eyes are bugging out again. Bad sign."

"Very bad sign."

"Madness will reign."

Roy grinned at us. "What we gotta do, we gotta boost a cow."

84

We stared at him.

"See? We boost the cow, take it to her place, wait for rain—"

"No *way,* Roy," I said. "I reject the idea."

"Ditto," said Scott.

"We're not boosting a cow," I said. "Turn up your hearing aid and listen hard: *we are not boosting any cow anywhere anytime."*

Suddenly the kitchen door swung open with a swoosh and Harvey entered, looking very evil and very crazed.

"Where the hell have you been all night? he said, glaring at Roy.

"What do you mean?"

Harvey was tapping a foot nervously and trembling at the same time. Then with a hissing sigh, like air escaping from a balloon, he sank into a chair.

"You know a couple of dinosaurs named Gallo? A deaf one and a big, stupid, vicious one? Well, they just happened to stop by last night to beat your brains out."

"Gallo?" Scott gaped at Roy, open-mouthed. "Aren't those the guys you work with?"

"What are they doing here, Roy?" I said. *"Roy,* what the hell are they doing out here?"

Roy looked almost embarrassed—a real rarity for him. "I sort of . . . Well, what happened was, I borrowed some cash for the trip."

Scott slapped his own face, a strange habit he had when upset. "You stole their money? Oh, my God!" The old Howdy Doody lower lip began to tremble.

"It ain't really their money."

"They must want it back pretty badly to wax your skull in another state," I said.

Harvey raised both hands to shut us all up. "Let me give you a little rundown on things, nephew. And it's all bad. First, I get a call last night from your dad. He's hysterical. These two goons showed up at his garage yesterday morning asking your whereabouts. No—*demanding* your whereabouts. One of them, your dad could see the bulge under his jacket. So he gives them my address. Then I go to a screening last night, and I come home and sack out. Around three in the morning I wake up staring up at these two goons. And they ain't pretty, either. The one that can talk wants to know where his money is. The other one—the deaf one—does the sign language bit, and when I surface from under the sheets they see I'm not you. But they're very, very interested in locating your ass—and I mean *now*. To make that point crystal clear, the idiot who talks grabs me by the neck and shakes me till my teeth rattle. Then the deaf one—Arturo—grabs me and shakes me. They threaten to break up my face—including my nose. My thousand-dollar nose! They so much as touch my schnozz, Roy, and I'll kill you, I swear to God."

When Harvey first started speaking Roy looked

cocky, then nonchalant, but by the end of his uncle's speech he was beginning to look kind of peaked and miserable.

"Jeez, Harvey, I never dreamed this was gonna happen."

"They said to tell you if you give them back their money you can keep your thumbs."

"I can't believe you stole money from the Gallo brothers," Scott said. All the color had drained from his face. He seemed to be in deep shock.

I ran the flat of my hand along Roy's neck, knife-slashing style. "You've signed your own death warrant," I said.

He tried to show a little of the old spirit—or moxie, as he liked to call it. He said, "Hey, in a couple days I'm gonna be in the army, surrounded by a million guys with guns. What are the Gallo brothers gonna do?"

"Roy," Harvey said, "do yourself and the family a big favor. Don't have any kids. I look at you and figure the Darpinian line must be running dry."

The situation between Roy and the Gallo brothers was far worse than even Roy suspected, though of course we didn't know it at the time. They had orders to either return the money Roy had stolen or make mincemeat out of him. I guess I'd led a pretty sheltered life up to that point because I'd never actually seen anyone made mincemeat of, and I hadn't given much thought to how you'd go about doing it. But I had the horrible feeling I was about to find out.

For the moment, Scott and I were willing to believe Roy when he assured us we could easily stay one step ahead of them. Our thoughts were again trained on Marilyn. She *had to know* we were more than just three adolescent nitwits at the end of her driveway.

After we had devoured half the groceries at Harvey's we drove back to Marilyn's house, again parking down the street where we couldn't easily be seen and yet would still have a clear view of her if she surfaced. About a minute after we arrived, two beautiful girls in T-shirts and shorts biked past the car.

"I'll tell you somethin'," Roy said. "Women are gonna be around a lot longer than anyone ever expected. That's a fact."

"What a moronic statement," Scott said. "It makes no sense."

I laughed. "Roy, you know what you are? You're ten pounds of shit in a five-pound bag."

"I'd just like to know what you two pea-brains are gonna do when I'm gone. Who's gonna keep you up on the latest nookie developments?"

"Come off it," I said. "You're not the only source on women anymore. That was fine when we were kids, but I'm eighteen now. My body has been fondled by hands that are not my own."

"And I'm getting married next month," Scott put in.

"A lot of good that's gonna do. The blind leadin' the blind."

"Says who, Darpinian?" That Howdy Doody lower lip started to grow thick.

"Dood," I said, "everybody knows you've been carrying the same rubber around in your wallet for three years."

"Two virgins," Roy said. "What a sad situation that is."

"Yeah, well, whatever Becky and I need to know we'll get it from each other."

"What a laugh. Women can't give the real stuff. They don't have it to give."

"Now just what the hell is *that* supposed to mean?" I said.

I was getting angry; I couldn't stand it when he got on Scott's case and wouldn't stop ragging him.

"Basically, women don't know nothin' worth knowin'."

"Darpinian," I said, "your mother soured you. She fucked you up. You really hate women, you know that?"

The mention of his mother shut him up, and an awkward silence followed.

"What time is it?" said Scott, who didn't have much tolerance for aggravation or tense silences. In his house everybody was always chatty and cheery.

"Two-oh-nine," I said as always.

Scott smiled. "Oh, yes, right. Two-oh-nine. Who could be in there with her?"

"If we just boosted a cow . . ." Roy said.

Right then the door to Marilyn's house opened and three people came out—a woman we'd never seen before followed by a man with a black beard, sunglasses, and an L.A. Dodgers baseball cap. Bringing up the rear was a woman with black hair and purple aviator glasses. The three of them entered a convertible that was parked in the driveway.

"Jesus," I said, "that's gotta be her."

"Who?" Scott said. "Which one?"

"I don't see no blonde," Roy said.

"The black hair and the shades. It's a disguise. She uses it on jerks like us."

Roy gave me a disgusted raspberry. "Forget it. That isn't her."

"I'm telling you, it is. Wait a minute." I opened my Marilyn Bible and started searching for a photograph.

"You're cracked, Bleuer. That ain't her body. That ain't the way she walks."

"Yeah? Well, what about this." I started reading from the Bible. "'She prowls the streets of New York sometimes in a black wig and a kerchief with no makeup on. But what most gives her away are the huge aviator glasses she adds to this disguise.'"

"Follow that cab, driver," Scott said with a grin, giving Roy a shove from the backseat.

We stayed close to the convertible without being noticed—Roy was getting good at it—tailing them west to Santa Monica and finally ending up at this beach—and it wasn't just any old beach, either. It was a nude beach!

"I can't believe this is happening to me," Scott said. "Pinch me. Wake me from my dream."

Old Roy jumped out of the car and began undressing. "Nobody's more fun than a naked woman. I mean *no*body."

I shook my head. "This isn't my scene. I have enough trouble getting naked in front of a mirror."

"Me, too," Scott said.

"We've managed to trap her here," Roy said. "Where can she go? It's a wide open beach. There's no place to run."

"Except across the water," I said.

"Hey, she's good, but she ain't no Jesus."

"I can't do it, Roy," said Scott. "I just can't take my clothes off."

"You wanna see her buck naked head to toe, Dood?"

"Well, sure. But why do we have to get naked? Why can't we just walk out there like this?"

"It's a nude beach, stupid. She ain't gonna respect us if we don't ask her out bare-assed. If we go out there in our civvies, she's gone.

"Where's she gonna run?" I said.

"Look, if you two mice wanna stay here playin' pocket pool, I'll go by myself. It don't matter to me."

Scott and I stared at Roy as he leaned against the fender of the Galaxie, as naked as the day he was born. The tattoo on his right buttock cheek said, "Born to raise hell." Slowly we began to undress.

With a wink in our direction, Roy crept up to a parked car with an open window, reached inside, and grabbed a large beach towel and a pair of sunglasses. He threw the towel to Scott who was slowly and reluctantly removing his clothes.

"Thanks, Roy," he said, "even though you swiped it." He wrapped it around his waist, draping it down to his ankles to hide his wooden leg.

We started walking along the beach, Scott in the towel, Roy in the sunglasses and me using my Marilyn Bible to hide my private parts.

The woman we figured was Marilyn's friend stood waist deep in the water. The woman with the black hair we figured was Marilyn—still wearing her aviator glasses and nothing else—waded out to stand beside her. The three of us stumbled through the sand, drinking up the sight of the numerous naked women all around us.

Scott's neck seemed to be on a swivel. "I've died and gone to heaven," he muttered.

"Jesus," I said, "do you realize we're gonna meet

her? In a minute we're actually gonna *meet* her. And in the buff—can you believe it?"

"I think I need to lie down for a minute," Scott said. "I'm feeling kinda dizzy."

"Too much for you, eh, Dood?" Roy laughed and gave Scott a goose through the towel.

Scott collapsed onto the sand, face down. I sat beside him, my Bible over my crotch, and Roy kept his attention riveted on the black-haired woman.

"Hey, Roy, you know what you're gonna say to her?" asked Scott.

"'You wanna go canoeing, baby?' is what I'll say, only I'll say it with my eyes. I got this thing I worked up with my eyes. One look and she's a quivering bowl of Jell-O."

"Oh, man," I said. "In other words, we've come all this way, and you haven't devoted one iota of your brain to this, have you? You don't have an idea in hell what you're gonna say."

"You just watch, Bleuer, you cretin. Watch and listen. You might learn something."

As the black-haired woman walked from the surf to her towel and lay on her stomach to dry off, old Roy strolled up to her, leaned down, and removed his glasses. We trailed after him to take in the action up close.

"Hello there," he said in this low, seductive voice he must have practiced in secret. It was enough to make me gag. "Now, my faithful companions here say they're gonna murder me for sayin' this to you, but I think you're a woman who can understand when I say I just wanna lay on top of you and see where it goes from there."

I felt like dying on the spot, and poor old Scott looked like he was in the middle of cardiac arrest, his hand clutching his heart and all and his face the color of dirty soapsuds. The black-haired woman turned over slowly and stared up at Roy. Then she removed her sunglasses. She was not Marilyn—and not only was she not Marilyn, the expression on her face was the expression of a girl who's just been surprised to find a huge cockroach in her bed.

"Get lost, pud," she said.

Roy gaped down at her. "Who the hell are you?"

"Who the hell are *you*, creep?"

Right then Roy looked down the beach, turned a few shades paler, and whispered, "Oh, shit, look what's here."

"What?" Scott and I said at the same time, too surprised at the urgency in Roy's voice to call a Jinx.

"This beach has just gotten very small," he said.

Marching toward us—most definitely not naked but with their pant legs rolled up—were the Gallo brothers. They saw us, they were headed straight toward us, and they were not smiling.

Roy started running toward the water's edge, and Scott and I were not far behind.

Eleven

"I can't swim," Scott said.

"If you guys ever thought about followin' me anywheres, now's the time."

"I can't swim," Scott yelled.

"I guess you're about to learn, Dood." And with that, Roy dived into the surf and started splashing wildly away from shore. Scott and I reluctantly followed and I protected my Marilyn Bible by holding it over my head and doing the dog paddle with one arm.

The Gallo brothers approached to the point where the sand got damp, but not an inch farther. Thank God they showed not the slightest passion for water.

"Roy," Antonio yelled in his gangster's growl, "you can't stay out there forever."

Behind the Gallos we saw a woman with black hair remove her wig and shake out her familiar blond mane.

Scott yelled, "Oh, my God, there she is!"

Once again we had missed her by a matter of inches.

"Man, what is this? Are we cursed or what? moaned Roy.

Roy and I paddled around and Scott walked out until the water was up to his neck.

"Hey," I said, swimming up close to Roy, "what the hell's going on? Did you steal their money or what?"

"Talk to you later."

"Now," I said. "This might be a really good time to give it back to them."

"Oh, right," he said. "You mean the money I deposited up my ass."

"I hate you, Roy," Scott said. "I hate you. You'll never know how much I hate you."

"Relax."

"First you get me naked, then you get me drowned and you're a crook. This isn't fun anymore."

"I wonder how they found us," I said.

"It don't matter," said Roy. "They found us."

"But why are Ned and I out here?" Scott said. They're only after you. We didn't do anything."

"Dood, these Gallos ain't really bad guys, but

they're morons and they play for keeps. They'll rip your leg off and beat you to death with it, just to get to me. If you're with me, you ain't innocent. Not to those Mongoloids."

"So how long would you estimate we're gonna be out here?" I said. "A week? A month?"

"That's a toughy. There's only two things that'll slow them guys down. Either they die or they get hungry."

"Which is more likely to happen in our lifetime?" I asked.

A wave crashed over us, knocking all three of us off our feet. Roy and I bounced right back up, but Scott was kicking and thrashing and gasping for air.

"Help! Help, Ned!"

Roy, a much stronger swimmer than I was, dove for him, and I followed, all thoughts of my Marilyn Bible gone from my head. Just as we got to Scott another wave crashed over us. For one awful moment we couldn't find him.

Roy came up from a dive, gasping for breath, and said, "Ain't wood supposed to float, for crissake?" Not waiting for an answer he went under again and this time he came up holding a shaking and choking Scott.

"Oh, God, oh, God," he said, gagging up some water.

"Dood, take it easy," Roy said, slamming him a good one on the back. "Breathe, man. Breathe."

"You okay, Dood?" I said. "Everything working?"

"Yeah—better." He coughed and then broke out in a big grin. "You know something? I was actually swimming there for a minute."

When I righted myself, I saw my Marilyn Bible floating a few feet away. *"Shit!"* I swam over and rescued it. It was totally messed up, particularly my notations in ink. I pressed it to my forehead and mumbled, "Thank you, Lord, for letting Marilyn stay with us instead of sinking into the briny deep."

The Gallo brothers just wouldn't go away. We stayed out in the surf, diving every time a big set of waves rolled in and getting colder and more miserable by the minute.

"Ghosts, men," Roy said.

"Okay," said Scott.

"F," said Roy.

"F-u," I said.

"F-u-c," said Scott.

"I quit," Roy said.

Suddenly Arturo, the deaf brother, was sniffing the air, jerking his head quickly back and forth like a dog on the scent of something. He signed to Antonio, who nodded, and they moved down the beach toward an area where there were stores and all.

Dying would have been a more permanent solution to our problem, but at least they did get hungry. Even out in the Pacific Ocean we could catch the exciting aroma of fried chicken with barbecue sauce; I was almost tempted to give up and join the Gallo brothers for some chow.

Once the coast was clear we waded into shore and hightailed it to the car, shivering like madmen. Scott and I dressed in about two seconds flat, but old Roy—ever the showman—had to comb his hair and light a cigarette first. We were all hungry, tired, scared, cold and thoroughly pissed off.

I slammed the Marilyn Bible on the seat beside me. "Goddamn it, I spent six years putting this collection together. It has all the *Life* articles ever written about her. Some of these pictures, I haven't seen them anywhere else. Now the whole goddamn thing is—"

Roy cut me off: "Will you clam up about your stinkin' Bible already?" He crushed out his cigarette and slowly started to get dressed, acting like he wasn't cold, but I could see he was shivering just like Scott and me.

I watched him, feeling a sudden rush of frustration and anger. "How much money did you steal, Roy?" I said.

"Borrow, you mean."

"Whatever. How much did you take?"

"A thousand bucks."

"A thousand?" Scott stared at him, his mouth hanging open. "Are you crazy? What were you thinking? No wonder the Gallo brothers are out to kill you. A thousand's big money."

"It's not theirs," Roy said. "I borrowed it from Herb Black. And by the way, how do you think we've been living so royally out here? On box tops? I've been spending, you've been freeloading. Do you think I minted the money down in the basement?"

"Oh Jesus!" Scott said, burying his head in his hands. "Worse and worse."

I guess this is the time and place to explain something about my buddy Roy. He told everybody he was working as a mechanic at a garage in Mercury, a small town near Indian Springs. But Scott and I knew he was a bagman for a bookie out of Las Vegas. To help him with his collections there were these two Mafia goons, Arturo and Antonio Gallo. I could just see the two of them putting old Roy against a wall in a dark alley, and the two of them furiously using sign language to decide his fate. If anything, all that hand and finger stuff made them seen even more menancing.

But messing with Herb Black was even stupider. He owned this big junkyard on the outskirts of Indian Springs, and he was no guy to cross. I'd worked for him once or twice; he was as tight as they come. He was a big-time gambler in Vegas, and everybody knew he had real close Mafia connections. Stealing from the Gallo brothers was one thing—broken bones maybe—but stealing from Black was more like planning your own suicide.

"You'd better explain this a little more carefully, Roy," I said. "Spell it out so I can understand. I mean, we're in this too, you know. If you're in hot water, so are we."

"I can't believe this," Scott moaned.

"Well, the real deal is, Herb won a bet. I was supposed to deliver his winnings with the Gallo brothers, but I told them I'd take care of it myself. The boys drove me to the junkyard in their fancy Lincoln. They started to get out and I said to them, 'You two don't gotta babysit me. Why don't you hang out, relax? I'll make the drop.' Antonio was a little nervous about it. Zanetti, my Vegas boss, he doesn't like any of us to make a drop alone. But I managed to sweet-talk old Antonio. I took the lunch bag filled with Herb's money and walked into the junkyard. Darlene was working behind the counter. She told me Herb was out back stacking hubcaps. So I went out, but instead of saying anything, I ducked around the corner and counted the money in the sack. A thousand and change. It went into my pocket and the sack in the trash. King for a day, man, that's how I felt. So I went back to the Lincoln and said to the boys, 'Ca'mon, men, let's eat this town to the ground.'" Roy spread his arms and smiled as if he'd just pulled something incredibly smart instead of incredibly stupid and dangerous.

"So you didn't deliver a single dime to Black," I said. "You kept it."

"Smart boy. You go to the head of the class."

"Roy, you're an idiot. Do you know that? You're crazy, man. You're gonna get killed. You can't mess with Black. He's sicced those Dobermans—the Gallo brothers—on you. It's simple: They get the money, every penny of it, or they get you."

"And maybe us," Scott said.

"Don't worry—things'll work out," Roy said. "I'll think of something. Right now the thing we gotta concentrate on is we have to boost a cow. It's our best chance to get to Marilyn."

"Forget the damn cow, Darpinian," Scott said. "Just for*get* it. I wanna go home. Becky's gotta be going nuts about now."

"Dood, I ain't gonna say this again, so listen close. We go home when I say we go home."

"Fine. Then I'll just take the car when you're asleep."

"Yeah, and who's gonna drive it?"

"I am."

"Who's gonna pump the gas pedal?"

"Who do you think?"

"You're nuts. You got born with the wrong leg, Dood."

That cruel comment cut Scott severely and was

followed by one of the longest and most awkward of our long, awkward silences. Roy was actually blushing with embarrassment, and to cover himself he started to slip his shirt on over his head. When his arms were raised, Scott removed the wad of bubble gum from his mouth and quickly shoved it into Roy's exposed armpit. He then forced Roy's arm down to make sure the gum would stick nice and fast.

"We're going home, dickhead," said Scott, sounding mean and very un-Dood-like.

"You son of a *bitch*," roared Roy. He turned to me. "Can you believe he stuck gum in my—"

"We're going home."

The thing is, you never want to get nice guys mad. When they get mad they go crazy; Roy had known Scott long enough to know that.

"Foreman," he said, "your ass is grass."

"I have a life ahead of me, you stupid prick, and I wanna be there for it."

"Yeah, well, you can't rub Ben-Gay on a heartache."

". . . Ben-Gay on a heartache," Scott said at the same moment and yelled, *"Jinx!"* He smiled proudly, having actually jinxed old Roy; it might have been the first time in his life. I couldn't recall another.

Roy said, "Listen up, asshole. You better figure out a very quick way to get this gum out of my armpit."

Out went Scott's lower lip. "I said, 'jinx.' You have to be quiet."

"Screw jinx," Roy said.

"But, Roy, I caught you. You know the rules. I caught you, man."

"So what you gonna do about it? You gonna make me shut up? Come on, Dood. Make me." He gave Scott a hard shove. "Come on—lay me out. Show me you got some guts."

"Come on, Roy," I said. "Lay off."

"Don't butt in, Bleuer. This is between the Dood and me." He shoved Scott again, even harder. "Let's see you get good and pissed, boy. Make a fist. You know how to make a fist? Your daddy ever show you how? I know you wanna turn my lights out."

"Roy, stop," said Scott.

"Roy," I said.

Roy punched Scott on the chest, and it wasn't a love tap either. "How can you stomach this? Punch me. Hit me so hard I'll have to take off my pants to brush my teeth. Does Becky know what a gimp mouse she's getting?"

The word "gimp" was what did it. "You bastard!" Scott lunged forward, pushed Roy out of the car, and jumped on him. They rolled around while Scott punched him around the face and neck, and Roy just took it. He made no effort to defend himself. I felt sick—sick for both of them, my two best friends—but I didn't know what to do. It was one of those times you seem to be outside yourself and you're paralyzed.

Scott kept whaling on him, and Roy said, "Harder. In the face again. All right—go for the gut. Harder. You hit like a chick."

Scott picked up the pace, and pretty soon Roy's face was a bloody mess. Finally Scott ran out of steam; he stared down at Roy who was wiping blood from his nose and mouth.

"Jesus, Roy . . . sorry, man."

"It's okay."

"I'm really sorry."

"I had it comin'. You gave it to me good, Dood. That's how it goes."

Scott and I helped Roy up from the ground.

"You're a mess, Darpinian," I said, and grinned.

He managed to grin back, and then after a minute Scott started grinning himself.

We were pretty quiet on the drive back to Harvey's house. I took the wheel for the first time on the trip; Roy was feeling on the rocky side. He sat in the passenger's seat, his left hand digging into his shirt trying to remove Scott's gum from under his arm. Scott sat in back staring out the window. You might have thought we were returning from a funeral or something.

When we got to Harvey's, Roy immediately

perked up. Harvey started to bawl him out all over again, but Roy put his arm around Harvey's shoulders and calmed him down. After some intense discussion between the two of them out by the pool, Harvey stormed out of the house looking excited, and Roy returned to the kitchen. He got real busy setting out a large spread on the dining room table. Scott and I couldn't believe it when he heaped a mountain of roast beef on a platter and put it out—"For the brothers," he told us.

"But we bought that for Harvey," I pointed out. "You know, for letting us stay here."

"Forget about it," said Roy. He explained, as he had at the beach, that the only thing that would stop the Gallo brothers was death or hunger, and he wasn't about to bet on death.

Apparently, if you believed Roy, the Gallo brothers were a couple of human garbage cans who'd never met a food they didn't like. But how stuffing their faces was going to get them out of our lives—that was hard to figure. So I said, "I don't see how laying out a spread of food's gonna solve anything. I mean, how's that gonna solve anything?"

"Trust me. I never finish something I don't start."

Scott and I stared at him.

"Now, what does that mean?" asked Scott. "You sure you got a handle on that cliché?"

"What time is it?" Roy asked me, ignoring Scott.

"Two-oh-nine."

Scott said, "Why do you bother to ask him, Roy?"

Roy looked out the window, and I thought I could sense some serious nervousness under his cool. "One thing about the brothers," he said. "They're always on time when it's time to pulverize somebody."

Scott squirmed in his seat. "Is anybody here getting pulverized tonight?"

"I don't wanna say nothin' more. I've got a choice plan, but it's better if I don't say nothin'."

"You're gonna give them their money back—right, Roy?" Scott slapped his forehead. "Hey, great plan. Give them all you got and promise to pay back the rest the minute you can. Wonderful! I'm one hundred percent behind it."

"There ain't no point to that. They want it all, and they want it now. What do you figure we been spendin' on this trip?"

"I don't want to know," Scott said.

"Maybe if you give them back the unused portion of their money," I said, "they'll let us keep the unused portion of our lives."

"You love to hear yourself talk, don't you Bleuer?"

We heard a car pulling up in the driveway.

"On the dot," said Roy. "Look—one thing I forgot. With the Gallos, any gunplay just duck for cover."

"Shit, Roy," I said, and Scott backed up right in step with me—a dance team, the two of us.

The doorbell rang. Roy walked slowly to the door and opened it. The Gallo brothers stood there, backlit by the sun, and they looked about as happy as they'd looked at the beach. Not happy.

"Antonio, Arturo," said Roy, "what a pleasant surprise. Come in, come in."

The Gallos entered, and I thought Antonio looked a little surprised by Roy's friendliness and apparent lack of fear.

"Thanks for using the door, boys," Roy said. His wit—if that's what it was—was lost on the brothers. "Hey, guys," he said to Scott and me, "look who's here for a visit."

Antonio leveled a flat gaze on Roy. "This ain't no visit."

"It isn't?"

"You're a hard kid to track down."

"Not really," Roy said. "You're just easy guys to shake, you know what I mean?" He gestured toward the table. "You hungry? The potato salad's terrific. So's the roast beef and rolls. Sesame. I'll bet you love sesame rolls, don't you, Antonio?"

Antonio didn't change his expression, and he didn't seem to salivate at the mention of food. "It was an awful thing you did, Roy, takin' that money. Very, very stupid."

"I feel terrible, and believe me, I hate puttin' you guys on the line like this, but . . . well, what can I say?" Roy shrugged. "I don't got your money. I'm tapped, man. No alibi. So how 'bout you just eat up, enjoy yourself, and then wax me? That a deal?"

Antonio signed Roy's explanation to Arturo, who signed back furiously. Then Antonio said, "You understand, we don't want to harm you. We've gotten along good up till now. But we gotta do what we gotta do. We got orders."

"Hey, I ain't complainin'. Do you hear me complainin'? You wanna bust me up, go for it."

Arturo signed to Antonio, who nodded in agreement and then said to Roy, "My brother says we will have to break all of your fingers and maybe one of your legs." Arturo signed again, and Antonio interpreted. "We will try to break them in places that are easy to mend."

"That's fair," Roy said.

"Roy . . ." Scott said.

"Uh, Roy," I said, "you're not going to let them do this to you, are you? There's something else, right? There's got to be something else."

Roy looked at me with a sad smile. I guess you could call it a resigned smile. It was a smile that scared me shitless. "These guys break bones," he said. "That's their job, and I'm their current assignment."

"Run, Roy," I said. "You don't seem to have a better plan."

Roy waved at the table, laden with food. "Are

you sure you don't want somethin' to eat first?" he said to the brothers. "To build up your strength?"

"We don't want nothin'."

"Come on, force yourselves."

Right then there was a loud banging on the door. Everybody jumped a mile in the air, except Arturo who was facing the kitchen.

"Police officers," we heard a deep voice yell. "Open up."

Antonio signed to Arturo, who reached inside his jacket, but while his hand was still fishing around in there in the folds of blubber, two cops entered quickly, their guns drawn.

"All right," said the thin cop, who had an even deeper voice than the fat cop who had yelled for us to open up, "you three boys up against the wall and spread 'em."

"This isn't happening," I said.

We lined up, and the fat cop frisked us while the thin cop kept his gun trained on us.

"What did we do?" Scott wailed.

The thin cop said, "Roy Darpinian, Scott Foreman, and Ned Bleuer, we have a warrant for your arrest for loitering, trespassing, and compound aggravation of a Miss M. Monroe at her residence."

"No," said Scott, violently shaking his head.

"That's not possible," I said.

Scott started whimpering. "She wouldn't do that to us. I just know she wouldn't."

"The complaint was filed this morning," said the

thin cop, who definitely seemed to be the mean one if they were playing the good cop–bad cop game.

"They're clean," said the fat cop when he finished frisking us.

"Cuff 'em."

After we were handcuffed, the thin cop glanced over at the Gallo brothers. "What are you two doing here?"

After signing to Arturo, Antonio said, "My brother and I, we're just here visiting our old friend Roy." He flashed Roy a yellow and completely unconvincing smile.

"Beat it," said the thin cop.

"What?"

"I said beat it. Does deafness run in the family?"

Roy rattled his cuffs together. "You can't hold us. We're only eighteen. We're juveys."

"Under California law you're adults," said the fat cop. "You're accountable for your actions."

"And you can get locked up with the big boys," added the thin cop with a leer. "The guys who love young things like you."

Suddenly we heard "Roy? *Roy?*" and Harvey came bursting through the door. "Oh, Jesus, *now* what?"

"Who in hell are you?" said the thin cop.

"Harvey Darpinian. I live here."

"Can you prove that?"

"Prove what? What do I have to prove? I *live* here. My initials are on the *door*mat. What's going on here?"

"These men are under arrest, and I'd advise you to calm down a little."

Harvey swung around to stare at the Gallo brothers, and his lip curled. "Oh, you two again. I'm not surprised."

"Not them," said the thin cop, and pointed at Roy, Scott, and me. "These are the J.D.'s. Why do ya think they're handcuffed—for kinky sex games or something?"

"Them?" said Harvey, stepping toward the officers. "You're arresting *them?* For what?"

"Stand back, please, sir," said the fat cop, his hand creeping toward his holster.

After a quick signing session with Arturo, Antonio edged toward the door. "We'd like to leave now if that's okay. But first we'd like to shake hands good-bye with our friend Roy."

"No!" Roy yelled, and everybody turned toward him. "This is horseshit, Harvey. They can't bust us. We don't live in this state."

"Shut up, Roy," I said. "Shut *up.*"

Making a weird animal sound, Roy leaped forward, grabbed the fat cop's gun from his holster, and pointed it at the two officers.

"Oh, God, oh God," moaned Scott, covering his eyes.

"Son . . . put that gun down," said the fat cop.

"If you wanna get in touch with me," said Roy, waving the gun around wildly, "talk to Uncle Sam."

As Roy quickly headed for the door, the thin cop pointed his gun at him and said, "Stop or I'll shoot. . . . I said, stop—" His gun discharged. Roy crumpled into a heap on the floor, blood beginning to trickle from his mouth.

"Holy hell," said the fat cop. "Ken?"

"It just went off, Pete," said the thin cop. "By itself . . . I swear. I swear I didn't . . ."

The fat cop knelt down to feel for Roy's pulse.

"I can't believe this," Scott said. He began yanking at his hair. "I can't *believe* this."

"Roy," Harvey said, rushing up beside his nephew. *"Roy."* Tears filled his eyes and began to leak down his face.

"I'm not getting a pulse," said the fat cop. "Ken, you better get an ambulance here."

The thin cop continued to stare at his gun and did not move. He looked as though he didn't know exactly where he was. "It just went off, Pete," he said again.

"Ken! Come on, man!"

The thin cop moved like a sleepwalker over to the phone and began dialing. His eyes were jumping all over the place like a crazy person's. Harvey knelt over Roy's limp body.

As for me, all I could hear was the reckless banging of my heart.

Edging closer to the door, Antonio cleared his throat and said, "Is he alive, Officer?"

The fat cop looked up grimly. "You and your

brother there, take a hike. And the two of you," he said, with a glance at me and Scott, "stay where I can see your faces."

Harvey cradled Roy's lifeless form, tears dripping from his face onto his nephew's.

"The ambulance is on its way," said the thin cop.

I must have been really out of it, because I didn't remember hearing him say a word on the phone.

The fat cop grabbed Roy's wrist and felt for a pulse. "It's too late."

"No," Scott screamed. "Jesus, *no!*"

"It just went off, Pete," said the thin cop, staring at nothing in particular. "I don't know what happened."

Antonio gently opened the front door. "We are sincerely sorry," he said, "speakin' for my brother as well as myself. We didn't mean for any of this to happen like this. Please pay our respects to his father."

The Gallo brothers quickly departed, inching the door closed silently behind them.

Scott rushed to join the lamenting Harvey, who was bent over Roy. Kneeling awkwardly, Scott said, "Roy . . . why'd you have to . . ."

"Dood," Roy said, sitting up, "you're castratin' the shit out of me with your wooden leg."

Scott's mouth fell open. So did mine. I also think my heart stopped for a beat or two.

"You're—you're alive," Scott said.

"Not bad for a dead guy, huh? Being able to talk and all?"

"God damn you, Darpinian," I said, not knowing whether to laugh or cry or jump on him and start whaling away.

"What's the matter, Neddy boy? You rather have me dead?"

"Why didn't you tell us?" Scott said.

Roy shook his head, smiling. "They had to buy it all. Everything. You haven't exactly got a poker face, Dood."

"These guys aren't really policemen?" said Scott, staring at the two cops.

"Meet Ernie and Steve," said Harvey. "They're actor friends of mine—currently between assignments, as we like to say in the business. And by the way, don't everybody break into spontaneous applause for our performance."

Roy and Scott and I solemnly clapped, and we kept clapping for a long time.

"You guys were great," said Roy. "I mean *great*."

"You weren't so bad yourself," I told Roy as he released our handcuffs. "Maybe acting runs in your family—you and Harvey. But you could've said something."

"Yeah, Roy," said Scott.

"Let me give you guys a fact," Roy said. "I just want you to know this, okay? If a hood walked in this room right now with a gun and said, "I'm gonna blow one of you away. Which one's it gonna be?" you know what I'd say? I'd tell him to shoot me, without even thinkin'. One hundred percent me."

He looked at Scott and me; we looked at him. And the weird thing is, I believed him, and I think Scott believed him too.

"You coulda told us, you bastard," said Scott. "And what about the blood? How'd you do that?"

"Simple," said Harvey. "I used to do a lot of magic. It's the old ketchup trick. You can hide it in your cheek."

"Well," I said, "I guess what we've got to do now is, we've gotta boost a cow."

Roy turned to me and smiled. And old Scott, he just looked plain relieved that his buddy was alive.

Twelve

Early the next morning we found the farm we were looking for. A fence ran along this big pasture filled with cows. Roy rolled down the window and inhaled. "Nothing like the smell of cow shit to kick off your day," he said.

"A cow's an amazing animal," I said. "I mean, how many other animals can turn grass into milk?"

"Yeah, Bleuer."

Scott looked up from the highway map he was studying and said, "This has to be the place Harvey was talking about."

"Listen," said Roy, "I say we just go on in and boost the cow."

"No stealing," I said. "We agreed on that."

"We're doing this honestly," said Scott, "or not at all."

"Look at all of them out there," Roy said. "The place is crawling with them. He ain't gonna miss one little old cow. Hey, there's a great-lookin' one right there."

"*No*, Roy," I said.

"Forget it. This time you listen to us," said Scott.

"Come on, guys, it's a piece of cake. Just hoist it over the fence, stuff it in the backseat and in two hours—two short, sweet hours—Marilyn's in our fingerprints."

"Think about the Galaxie," Scott said. "Think about your old man. You'd better believe you'd catch hell if you put a cow in his backseat."

"Cow shit and everything?" I added.

"He's had cows back there before."

"Human cows, maybe," said Scott. "Otherwise known as dogs."

"Look, Roy," I said, "which part of the word 'no' don't you understand? We *rent* the cow. Cow, trailer, the whole bit."

"We got plenty of money," Scott said.

"Fine, fine, we'll do it your way, then. But I'll tell you one thing right now. With the farmer I do all the talkin'."

Scott and I rolled our eyes at each other. It seemed like this was where we came in.

We drove up to the farmhouse, knocked on the door, and were told by a large lady in a flowered apron that the man of the house was out yonder by the chicken coops. So we went out yonder, near a big barn she pointed out, and Roy, sunglasses in hand, started right in on the farmer without so much as a "Hello, how are ya?"

"You want to rent one of my cows?" the farmer said about five times. He looked Roy up and down, and I wasn't all that sure he liked what he saw. "For what?" he said.

"About two, three hours."

"I mean how much money?"

Maybe the farmer didn't like Roy's looks or personality, but it was pretty clear that he did like money. We made the deal, and he helped us select a cow. Kind of a small and drab one, I thought, but a real live cow. The farmer claimed it was a special cow, but she acted like all the other cows as far as I could tell—you know, like a cow. She seemed pretty damn stubborn when we tried to push her up the trailer ramp.

"Come on, Bossy," Scott said.

"Try calling her another name," I said. "Something less degrading."

"What's wrong with Bossy? I had a dog named Bossy."

"I remember. I remember it bit you, too."

"Come on, Evelyn," Scott said.

I looked at him. "Your mother's name?"

"It's the first thing that popped into my head."

"Calling your mother a cow, Dood," said Roy, who strolled back to us after chatting with the farmer. "That ain't good."

I was interested to see if Roy would help us wrestle with the cow. He was never too keen on work when there was anybody else to do it for him.

We shoved with all our might, but the stupid cow still refused to budge. Roy urged us on, shouting directions, but I noticed he didn't lift a finger to help. When we stopped to catch our breath, Roy lit a cigarette and made faces at the cow.

"Don't scare the poor thing to death," I said.

"Why isn't that farmer helping us?" Roy said.

"'Us'? You said 'us,' Roy?"

"He's busy with the chickens," Scott said.

Roy paced up and down like a foreman on a chain gang. "He oughta be helping us."

Scott studied me. "I wonder if my face is as red as yours is."

"It's red, Dood."

"This is hard work."

"We need the damn farmer," Roy said. "He knows cows."

"Old Evelyn here ought to jump at the chance to meet Marilyn," I said.

"You know, I've been wondering," said Scott. "Why have we waited so long to get together with Marilyn? We've loved her for years."

"Search me," I said. "Maybe we weren't ready before. Maybe we were too immature. Not that we're all that mature now, but at least we're mature enough to recognize how immature we are."

"You sure love the sound of your own voice,

Bleuer," said Roy. "I'm really getting pissed off at that farmer. Where is he, anyway? He takes his money and runs." He went off to find him.

"I wanted Marilyn all to myself," Scott said. "Can you imagine *me* thinking that? There must be a hundred million guys who want her."

I looked at Scott, who seemed even more serious than his usual serious self. "You want her in what sense?"

"I know this is gonna sound corny, but when I see her I feel this feeling where my leg is—where it ought to be. I want to marry her."

"Hold up there a minute. What about Becky? You want 'em both?"

"God . . . Becky," Scott said. "You know I saw her face today in a cobweb?"

"In a what?"

"A cobweb."

"Yeah, right."

"Why did she let me come on this trip, Ned? She shoulda said no. What am I going to do?"

"About what?"

"I'm just not—I don't think we belong together."

"That's ridiculous. How can you even say that? You and Becky are perfect for each other."

Scott's lower lip grew thick—a bad sign. Tears might not be far behind. "It's like Roy was saying. What if she only loves me for my leg? This ugly piece of wood, my Howdy Doody face . . . she thinks she has to take care of me. Is that the right reason to get married?"

"It's up to you, Dood. You gotta decide what you believe is true."

"I don't know. . . . It's— Help me, Ned. Tell me what you really think."

"Dood, you're asking the wrong guy. The last right decision I made was— I don't know when."

Scott looked at me, started to say something, and then waited. I guess he could tell I was struggling with something on the heavy side.

"You know how everybody's so thrilled for me because I'm finally getting out of Indian Springs?" I said. "Well, I'm not going anywhere. When September comes I'll still be here."

"What do you mean? What about college?"

"Yeah, what about it? Harvard was important to my father. But why do *I* have to be so thrilled about it? I'm gonna die at Harvard. After the first semester I'll probably be back at the toy store. I don't know, I just— I wouldn't mind if once in a while someone asked me what *I* want."

I looked at the cow. "Okay, Dood, we've rested enough. We gotta move Evelyn. Your strength back?"

"Yeah."

"Let's do it." I approached the cow cautiously; I didn't sense any great affection on her part. "Come on, baby," I said, giving her what I hoped she took as a friendly slap on her flanks.

We pushed the stubborn Evelyn a few inches up the ramp. A minute or so later Roy came back with the farmer. He was talking a mile a minute. "The cow will listen to you, chief," he said. "You're the boss man. I paid you to get her up the ramp, so let's get her up there."

"You paid to rent the cow," said the farmer.

"Come on, have a heart. The beast'll listen to you."

The farmer, cursing under his breath, walked up to Evelyn and I swear he whispered something in her ear. It seemed to kind of flap as he talked. He touched her, made a little movement with his fingers, and the cow obediently moved up into the trailer. The three of us watched in amazement.

"Take good care of my cow," said the farmer. "And be back before sundown."

"Right, chief," said Roy, and we took off for Hollywood.

We spent the drive figuring out what we would say to Marilyn once we were actually with her.

"There's one line I like," Scott said. "'Marilyn, I'd walk a thousand miles through the burning desert just to help you on with your coat.'"

"Yuck," said Roy, pretending to puke out the window.

"You're sure gonna impress her with that line," I said. "Come on, Dood. She'll take you for a witless sap."

"Well, what if I just tell her the truth, then? 'I'm

sorry for all the trouble I've caused, Marilyn, but I just had to meet you once before I died.' How's that?"

Roy said, "Maybe you might wanna go back to 'Hi, I'm Scott Foreman. Thank you for talking to me.'" He laughed and banged on the steering wheel.

"Yeah, and what are *you* gonna say, Roy?" Scott said. "It better not be any of this 'I wanna lay down on top of you' stuff. You can't say that to Marilyn."

"You're right, Dood," said Roy, suddenly sounding serious and not his usual tough self. "I guess what I'm gonna say is, I'm gonna say, 'Marilyn, I love you. I love you more than I've loved any woman. I've waited for you longer than I've waited for any woman. I'm a man on my knees. . . .'"

Scott and I looked at each other and then at Roy. I guess we were shocked by his sudden attack of sincerity.

"Did you make that up?" I said. "It's not exactly vintage Darpinian."

"It's good stuff, right?"

"Yeah, but not original with you," Scott said. "I remember that from *Gone With the Wind.*"

"Well, yeah, but I made it better with the knee bit. The knees are my touch. They're a real killer, don'tcha think?"

Evidently the cow thought so, because right then she let out this earsplitting moo.

It was still pretty early when we got to Marilyn's house, and nothing was stirring. This was not a neighborhood where people left home at dawn with lunch pails. We got Evelyn out of the trailer, walked her across the street and up to the side of the house. Roy jimmied the lock on the garage door and found a garden hose inside. He attached it to an outside water pipe, and Scott made rain by holding his thumb over the end of the hose, causing water to spray into the air and all over Evelyn, who didn't seem to mind in the least. But again, for some reason, she refused to give us the kind of cooperation we'd paid good money for. No moos. Not a single, solitary moo now that we needed one. So Roy and I crouched in the shrubbery and began mooing our heads off.

"I feel like an idiot," Scott whispered. "The idiot rainmaker."

"Can it, Dood," Roy said.

"You wanna moo for a while?" I asked Scott.

"That's okay," Scott said. I'm not terrific at cow imitations."

So Roy and I went on making cow noises, a little louder than before, and because practice does make perfect we were really starting to get off some terrific moos. Then I noticed that the curtains—in what I figured was one of the rear bedrooms—were pulled back slightly, and I could see two heads peering out at us. It was too dark to distinguish whose heads they were, but I figured the housekeeper's and Marilyn's. Roy and I went on mooing, Scott kept the rain falling, and old Evelyn just stood around not contributing anything, and the faces in the window kept looking out and then one of them disappeared and reappeared at the front door. It was Mrs. MacDonald.

"All right, boys, enough is enough," she said. "Miss Monroe thinks you're very amusing, but this has to stop now. Do you hear me? You with the hose, cut off the water, and you two in the hedges—do you realize you're trampling on flowers?"

Miss Monroe thinks you're very amusing....

I stared at the window again, and maybe it was my imagination working in overdrive, but I thought I could see Marilyn smiling out at us. Then, to my horror, I saw Mrs. MacDonald heading right for me. I looked around for Roy, but he'd pulled a pretty swift vanishing act. I jumped up from the bushes and, for some reason, raised my arms above my head like some criminal.

Mrs. MacDonald pointed a finger at Scott. "Put the hose back in the garage, young man, and get this cow off the property immediately. He's eating the nasturtiums."

With her help—she was on the burly side and pretty strong—we managed to get Evelyn moving in the general direction of the trailer, but it wasn't easy. Scott stood in front, pulling on the cow's ears, I pushed from behind, and Mrs. MacDonald slapped the cow on its flanks. All the time I was wondering where the hell Roy had disappeared to.

"Push harder," Scott said, panting.

"You pull harder," I snapped back at him.

"I'm pulling as hard as I can. I don't think she enjoys having her ears pulled."

"If I push any harder, I'll be pulling," I said.

"That doesn't make any sense," said Scott.

"Miss Monroe wants this animal off her property," said Mrs. MacDonald, giving the cow a punch in the ribs.

Where was Roy? I wondered.

"Maybe you could come back here and help me push, ma'am," I said to Mrs. MacDonald, but she didn't hear a word. Her attention was drawn to the front door. "Oh good heavens," she yelled. "Oh, no!" She started running toward the house just as Roy strolled out on the porch, putting on his sunglasses and lighting a cigarette. He acknowledged Mrs. MacDonald with a wink and a grin. She rushed by him into the house, yelling, "Miss Monroe? *Miss Monroe?* Are you all right?"

"What happened?" Scott and I asked Roy at the same instant, but we were too excited to think of jinxing each other.

"Did you talk to her?" Scott asked.

"Let's get the cow in the trailer and get out of here," Roy said, and he wouldn't say another word until we shot away from 12305 Fifth Helena Drive.

"Well?" I said. "Come on, spill it, Roy."

"What did you say to her?" Scott said. "What did she say?"

"Well," Roy said slowly, "when the housekeeper came out to shoo us off the property, I just walked in the front door. Easy as pie. I walked through the living room and dining room and came to this closed door. I knocked and her voice—we've heard that voice a thousand times, haven't we?—her voice said, 'Yes, what is it?' "

"Were those her exact words?" said Scott.

"Shut up," I said to Scott. "Go on, Roy."

"I took her question as like an invitation, so I went in—in her bedroom. She looked kinda surprised but not scared or anything—"

"What was she wearing?" Scott said, his voice cracking and all atremble.

"Black slacks, a white sweater. Barefoot. So there we are starin' at each other and I say, 'Marilyn, Marilyn—how you doin'?' You know, like real casual? Then I say to myself, To hell with it, do what you gotta do, and I say, 'I love you, Marilyn, and I got this idea. This very excellent idea. What would you think about me just layin' on top of you and see where it goes from there?' "

By this point in the story we'd pulled up to Googie's coffee shop. We ordered hamburgers and fries, but for once we didn't have any appetite. Scott and I just stared at Roy like we'd never laid eyes on him before.

"You stupid shit," I said softly.

He nodded, shrugged, said nothing.

"Jesus, Roy, you didn't," Scott moaned. "You didn't *say* that. Tell me you're kidding."

"I ain't kidding, Dood."

"You said *that?*"

"Word for word. Just like I'm sayin' it to you now."

"I guess you're proud of yourself," I said.

"Not really. I just did what came naturally."

"And of course she said no. Right, Roy?"

He nodded and stared at his food.

"I mean what is she gonna say?" I went on. "A guy breaks into her house and starts this jazz about lying on top of her . . . Jesus, Roy, what do you expect?"

Roy looked at us with a little smile. "Well, just for the hell of it, I left Harvey's number."

"I'm sure she'll call," Scott said sarcastically.

"Tell me, lover boy," I said, "what were her parting words?"

"'Get lost.' That's all she said." Roy shrugged.

"She didn't say 'get lost,'" I said.

"Marilyn doesn't talk like that, Roy," Scott said. *"You* talk like that."

"She said 'get lost' or 'get out of here' or 'get off the bed.' I can't remember the actual words."

"I want to see the scene," said Scott. "Describe it for me. How did she look up close? Were her eyes half open, kind of sleepy? Did she ever close her mouth? What about that famous hip wiggle?"

Roy shrugged.

"Look, Roy, you gotta understand," I said. "You were with her. *You were right there with her.* We just want a complete account, that's all."

"The room was dark. She was just layin' there when I busted in. I gave her my best shot and that was it. She wasn't interested in old Roy. Hey, I don't cry over no woman, I don't care who she is."

A cold, ugly silence gripped the three of us. Scott pushed a french fry through some ketchup but couldn't bring himself to lift the fork to his face.

"We shoulda gone for Elizabeth Taylor," Roy said finally.

I looked up from my untouched hamburger. "You gotta be kidding."

"God, this is so depressing," Scott said. "We don't even deserve to be mice."

"Look, guys," I said, "just because we struck out with Marilyn doesn't mean we have to go home with nothing. We can still turn this trip around."

"Fat chance," said Scott.

Roy looked faintly interested. "Whaddaya got in mind?"

"We're forgetting where we are," I said. "Hollywood. The land of dreams. We've been here awhile now, and we're still on Marilyn's front porch. As far as I'm concerned the only thing that matters tonight should be us. We oughta be out there doing everything—everything we've never done before—and a few things we have done and wouldn't mind doing again." I took a big bite of my burger, even though I wasn't hungry. The funny thing is, once I took a bite I all of a sudden *got* hungry.

Thirteen

So that night we got decked out in our finest clothes and dragged the Sunset Strip in the Galaxie, which was all shined up and looking almost brand-new again, except for the fender.

To get into the spirit of the evening we went to this dance club and did the twist for about an hour. Old Roy paired off with this older woman—she was thirty if she was a day—and Scott and I danced across from each other. I tried to imagine he was Marilyn, which wasn't easy, having to look at him. Because of his wooden leg Scott's twisting was a little clumsy, kind of like the Tin Woodman doing a jig when he's a little low on the old oil, but you had to hand it to Scott for really trying.

Later on, after stuffing our faces with tacos and

stuff, we followed these humongous spotlights to Grauman's Chinese Theatre where a premiere was about to happen. A long red velour carpet was spread out on the walkway beneath the canopy from the curb to the entrance of the theater. Restraining ropes had been set up to keep the hundreds of eager dopes like us from molesting the arriving movie stars.

We hip-swiveled, body-checked, and shouldered our way up to the rope for a clear view. Because Roy was so short—something Scott and I were absolutely forbidden to discuss—he sat on Scott's shoulders, giving him the best seat in the house.

"Hey, look, there's James Darren," I said.

"Where? Where?" said Scott.

"He's coming up. See him?"

"Hey, Jimmy Darren!" Roy shouted. "Chief! I saw your last four movies. I want my three dollars back. *The Guns of Navarone* . . . too loud."

"Cool it, Roy," I said as Darren swept by, ignoring him.

"There's Dean Martin," said Scott.

"Hey, Dean," Roy yelled, wagging a finger. "Dino, over here, man. I saw your last four movies. I want my three dollars back. Find yourself another Jerry."

I thought I heard Dean mumble "Fuck off" under his breath, but I couldn't be sure with all the noise. People in the crowd turned to stare at Roy, some of them making angry comments.

"Shut up, Roy," I hissed at him. "These people don't appreciate your wit."

"So you think I care? We're never gonna see these droolers again."

"Oh, my God," Scott said, "is that Chubby Checker?"

"Holy shit!" I said. "What's he doing here?"

"Hey, Chubby," Roy shouted. "Give us a twist. Come on, Chubs."

As Chubby Checker was walking down the red carpet with a date, he paused and looked at Roy, who was singing "My daddy's sleepin' and Mama ain't around. We're gonna twister..." and doing his best to twist while propped up on Scott's shoulders. The crowd went wild when Chubby did a miniature twist and sang "Come on, little miss, and do the twist" before he moved on into the theater.

Roy howled with laughter as he slithered down off Scott's shoulders.

The crowd continued to grow, the stars continued to arrive, and suddenly Scott and I realized we'd lost Roy. We kept craning our necks looking for him, and missed a lot of the stars as they passed within feet—even inches—of us.

"What's that little bastard up to now?" I said. Then Scott gave me a nudge on the arm and pointed. There was Roy—*inside the rope*—right on the old red carpet, walking slowly toward the theater entrance alongside two elegantly dressed

Hollywood types. He had a cool attitude, just like a star, just like he belonged there. I couldn't help admire his guts. When he disappeared inside Grauman's, Scott and I pounded each other on the back and grinned. But we'd hardly gotten our little celebration started when Roy was escorted right back out of Grauman's by two burly uniformed ushers.

"Hey, I have a ticket," Roy cried indignantly. "Who keeps their ticket stub? I tossed it on the floor."

"We understand, sir," said one of the ushers, giving Roy a gentle but firm shove into the night.

"No wonder nobody comes here," Roy said, playing to the crowd. "It's so damn crowded. Wait'll I see my agent about this."

"That's really telling them, Roy," I said.

"You really told them, Darpinian," said Scott.

"Let's split," said Roy, and he grinned and waved at the crowd, still playing the star, as we left. He wasn't too bad at it either, to tell the truth.

Our next stop was a tattoo parlor, farther out the Strip toward the ocean. We sat in the waiting room leafing through a book filled with tattoo designs—animals, knives, big tits, you name it.

"This is where you make your stand, Dood," said Roy. "Do you or don't you?"

"Becky would throw a fit if she saw one of those on me."

"Put it someplace she'll never figure to look."

"Like where? She's gonna be my wife. In eighty years she'll know every square inch of my body."

"Get it on your pecker."

"You gonna get another tattoo, Roy?" I said. "You already got that one on your ass."

"Yeah, Roy," said Scott. "Born to raise hell. And ain't *that* the truth."

"My old man took me for that when I was ten, but he made me get it on my ass in case maybe one day I got sick of lookin' at it."

"Your father got you tattooed when you were ten?" I asked.

"I thought you were born with it. Kind of like a birthmark," Scott said, nodding.

"It was all up to me. After my mother split, my old man didn't care what I did. Hell, I don't even know why he kept me around. But that's okay. I don't have no more use for him than he has for me. I'm goin' places. People are gonna give me respect, listen to what I have to say."

"They're gonna kill you," Scott said. "Is that the only reason you joined up, because of your dad?"

"Maybe he wants you to stay," I said. "Maybe he just finds it hard to show it."

"Yeah, right. Every Saturday morning he made me step into the ring with him so he could hand me my ass, like I was the nearest thing to my mother he could punch."

"You know," said Scott, "it could be he hit you because it was the only way he could think to get through to you, show you he cares. You're not exactly an easy case, Darpinian."

"This ain't the goddamn 'Andy Griffith Show.' When I'm gone he ain't gonna miss me one stinkin' bit."

"Are you gonna miss him?" I had to ask.

Roy shook his head and stared down at his hand, which he'd balled into a fist. "He's a loser. If he had an ounce of guts he'da bought it in Korea like your old man, Ned. At least I'd respect him then—his memory."

I said, "Why do either of you have to die to let the other know you're still alive? Jesus, you have each other and you don't even . . ." I felt myself beginning to lose control; I wanted to stop, to change the subject, but some deep need seemed to drive me on. "I would give anything to have my father back for five minutes—just five lousy minutes, so I could talk to him. I have so many memories, but they're fading. I look at old photographs, I don't know who I'm looking at." I stared down at my hands. I couldn't stop the tears from coming.

"Hey, Bleuer, at least you know your old man loved you." Roy gave me a punch on the shoulder. "And he was a hero, so he gave you something to hang on to."

I looked at Roy and I didn't try to hide my tears. "Who *cares* if he was a hero? The thing is, he's dead. He's— I'll never be able to talk to him. I'll never know what was in his head, what he really felt about things. He'll never be here to tell me . . . to help me, you know, like what should I do? He told me to read the newspaper and know what's going on in the world. I remember that. I've been reading—I read the fucking newspaper every day—and why? For what? What am I supposed to do with everything I know, so many facts lined up in a row? The man's dead, and I—I need him. . . ."

Scott grabbed me and hugged me, and I really let the old tears come—tears that had been welling up inside me for years. Roy looked at Scott holding me and then looked away.

"You're all right, Bleuer," Roy said softly. "You're gonna be just fine."

I tried to grin, and once I started grinning I felt like grinning. When the tattoo guy finally got around to us we decided to get identical tattoos on our right legs—Scott's right leg was the wooden one. I said why not get hearts with Marilyn's face inside, and Roy said the heart ought to be cracked open with Marilyn's face coming through because she would break our hearts in the end. All women broke your heart sooner or later, he said. So the cracked heart was what we decided on and it turned out just terrific.

Fourteen

It was the middle of the night and I dreamed the phone was ringing, but how could it ring in the bomb shelter? Then I suddenly remembered we weren't there! We'd all felt kind of claustrophobic after a night inside thick layers of concrete and we'd talked Harvey into letting us sack out on the floor in the living room. I opened my eyes and the phone was ringing. Scott and Roy were sprawled on blankets, dead to the world. I stumbled over their bodies and picked up the phone.

"Hello," I said, yawning my head off.

"I'm trying to reach Roy Darpinian."

"Roy?" The fog was beginning to lift, and the voice on the other end sounded familiar, like it belonged to somebody I knew but didn't talk to much. "Who shall I say is calling."

"Marilyn Monroe," said the voice. "He gave me this number. I apologize for calling so late."

I stared at the phone in a state of total shock. Yes, it was her voice all right. "Marilyn Monroe?" I said stupidly. Holy shit, man, get a grip on yourself!

"If this is an inconvenient time I can call again."

"Oh, no. Oh, no, no—please. Just hang on a minute, I'll get him, Miss Monroe. Please hold on." I covered the mouthpiece and gave Roy a violent kick. "Roy, get up, get up! *Get up!*" I kicked him again. "It's Marilyn!"

"Wha . . . ? What the fuck you doin', kickin' me?"

"It's Marilyn Monroe—on the telephone. She wants to talk to you."

"Who?"

"Marilyn Monroe, you dumb bastard. Wake up."

"No shit? I don't believe it."

He started to rise, and Scott did too.

"If this is some joke," Roy said, "I'll kill you."

"It's no joke."

"Well, I told you, didn't I?" he said, grinning. "Didn't I tell you she'd come through?"

"I can't believe she's calling us," Scott whispered. He stared at the phone and at Roy with a look of childlike wonder.

I handed Roy the phone and said, "Be nice, man."

He cleared his throat and said, "This is Roy Darpinian." He listened for a minute. "Yeah, sure—a soft top. No sweat." He listened some more. "No, that's no problem. Give me twenty minutes—thirty minutes tops. I'll see you then." He hung up, then turned to us and grinned.

"Well?" Scott and I said at the same time, too excited to jinx each other.

"I think I'm about to go on a canoeing trip, boys."

"Whaddaya mean?" I said.

"She can't sleep. She says she's having a lot of trouble sleeping lately and she'd like to take a drive down the Pacific Coast Highway. She wondered if I'd like to pick her up and drive her around."

"Wow!" Scott yelled and did a little Tin Woodman jig. "Get dressed, man! Get going! Jump in the shower!"

"That's great, Dood," I said. "I love your sequence—'Get dressed, jump in the shower.'"

"I'm fine the way I am," Roy said. "I'll just slip on my pants and shoes and I'm off."

"Whoa, not so fast," I said. "The Dood's right. Take a shower and move the old soap around. You stink. And try brushing your teeth."

"We're cruisin' the highway with the top down. She ain't gonna smell anything." He started running around nervously. "Where the hell are my car keys?"

"At least do something about your breath," Scott said. "It could peel paint."

"My breath's fine."

"Yeah, fine if you're a goat." Scott reached into his pants, pulled out a stick of bubble gum and handed it to Roy.

"Maybe I could wear somethin' different," Roy said, and started drifting toward the bedrooms. Scott and I trailed after him. He opened Harvey's door and turned on the light. A startled and naked Harvey and Delphine shot up in bed, scrambling to pull blankets up over themselves. Ignoring them, Roy went straight to the closet and started pulling clothes out.

"Hey, hey," Harvey said. "Just what the hell do you think you're doing? This happens to be my bedroom, in case you—"

"Sorry, Unc," said Roy, "but I gotta have an outfit fast."

"Jesus, what time is it?"

I glanced at my watch and said, "Two-oh-nine. Roy's got a date with Marilyn—like right now."

"You mean he really got the date? You got it, Roy?"

"She just called."

"She called here? You actually got the date?"

"Twenty minutes, she'll be in my arms."

Scott and I helped Roy sort through Harvey's clothes. I'd never seen such a weird collection of designs and colors in my life; it was like he was auditioning for the circus.

"Harvey," I said, "don't you have anything from the planet Earth?"

"Take what you want," he said, sinking back in the bed, half over Delphine. "Be my guest. But don't criticize."

I grabbed a suit, and Scott and I followed Roy into the bathroom. He took a gargantuan handful of Vaseline and plopped it in his hair and started stirring it around.

"That's way too much," Scott said.

"Nah, it's just right."

"For a petroleum field," I said. I waved the suit at him. "Get undressed, and make it snappy. Let's not keep the lady waiting."

"You know, you might try some Q-Tips," Scott said as he examined Roy's ears.

"I'm late. I don't have time for all that stuff." He slapped his pants. "Where the hell are my keys. Oh, here they are." He dredged them out of his hip pocket and started for the door. I jumped in front of him, blocking his exit.

"I don't want you to screw this up, Roy. You're not getting out of here till you shower, shave, use deodorant, brush your teeth, change clothes, and go through a huge evolutionary change."

As he tried to move by me, I grabbed his T-shirt—seriously soiled—and ripped it down the front.

Roy stared at the shirt and then at me in disbelief. "Why'd you do that, Bleuer?"

"You're not wearing those clothes. Not to take Marilyn out, you're not." To make my point crystal clear, I ripped the shirt even farther, down to his waist.

The two of us locked stares. Finally he said, "How come the way I look never bugged either of you before?"

"Because you never went out with anyone we respected before," Scott said.

"Listen to me, Roy," I said. "Just *listen* for a change. It's not only you with her. It's us. It's Harvey."

"Harvey?"

"It's every guy you know. This is probably the most important thing you're ever going to do in your whole life. It will never be as good as this again. *Never.*"

Roy wrinkled his forehead, looking puzzled. "Jeez, it's only a date."

I shook my head. "Why did it have to be you? Anybody else—Scott, me. Anybody. You just don't understand."

Roy stared at me, and suddenly his shoulders seemed to slump. It was like someone had let the air out of him and he was deflating before our eyes.

"Fuck it, Bleuer. Why don't you take her?"

"Just get yourself together is all I'm asking."

"You take her."

"Roy, get serious. This is your date."

"All this standing around talking," Scott said. "Somebody's gonna be late. You can't keep her waiting."

Roy continued to stare at me. "She'll have a better time with you, Bleuer."

"How can I take her out? She called you. She made the date with you."

"Tell her I was the beard. I warmed her up. You go in and polish her off. She'll go for it."

"Seriously? You want me to take her?"

"She's waitin' for somebody. I only wanna canoe her, man. You're the one with the torch, the romance, or whatever it is. Hell, I say go for it."

So I shaved and showered and shampooed in about five minutes and put on the least flashy of Harvey's ensembles. It almost fit. After I got dressed, Roy presented me with his tapped twister shoes. They were half a size too small for me, but I didn't plan to do much walking.

"Thanks, Roy," I said. "I know how much you love these shoes."

"Something of me's gotta be there."

Scott looked me up and down and slowly nodded his approval. "God, I wish I was you tonight, Ned."

He and Roy went outside with me and watched me climb into the Galaxie and fire it up. I raced the engine a little and grinned, trying to pretend I wasn't nervous. "Well, here goes nothing. I hope I'm not back in ten minutes."

"You won't be," Scott said.

"How you feelin'?" Roy said. "Good and horny, I hope."

"I feel like I'm about to shit razor blades, if you wanna know the truth."

"Well," Roy said, "give her my best. And if she suggests a canoe trip, don't turn it down."

I waved and took off and watched them through the rearview mirror until I turned the corner. And then I was on my own—on my way to a date I'd waited most of my life for. On my way to see the calendar girl of my golden dreams.

Fifteen

When I pulled up to 12305 Fifth Helena Drive I started to park way down the street in our usual stakeout position before I realized that for the first time I was here on legitimate business. *I had a date with Marilyn Monroe.* Me, Ned Bleuer, high school graduate, class of '62, Indian Springs, Nevada! I parked right in front of the house, took a deep inhale for courage, cupped my hand over my mouth, and blew air up into my nose, checking my breath, then strolled up to the front door and rang the bell. This time when Mrs. MacDonald answered—and after the first ring, too—she smiled. I wondered what she was doing up in the middle of the night, but I didn't feel like having a long conversation with her about it. I followed her into the living room and sat on the forward two or three inches of the couch. She brought me a cherry pop and I held it in my hand and stared at it. The house was as silent as a tomb. The only sound was the fizzing of the carbonated bubbles in my glass.

A million times I must have played out this scene in my head—all the funny, inventive things I'd say, and the musical peal of Marilyn's laughter as she listened to me, appreciating my wit and intelligence. But the truth was, I'd be lucky to be able to finish my own sentences. I had this weird feeling that Marilyn was going to tell me something, that she had a message for me, an important message. I had no idea what it was. Maybe it was nothing, or not something you put into words. Maybe it would just be the fantastic sense of standing toe to toe with her and breathing in the same air. Out of all the billions of people on earth, Marilyn and I would share that earth, just the two of us, for at least an hour or two, listening to each other, looking at each other. Just the two of us, nobody else. What a fantastic idea that was! And I'd try to stretch that time, too, as far as it would go. I had to be near her for as long as she'd let me.

I knew whole scenes from her movies by heart. So did Roy and Scott. Sometimes we'd play different parts and speak the dialogue from the movies. One scene I loved was Tom Ewell's Rachmaninoff dream sequence from *The Seven Year Itch*. I could see Marilyn appearing at the door in a strapless gown smoking a cigarette while Tom played Rachmaninoff on the piano. As I sat there waiting for the real, honest-to-God Marilyn to appear in the flesh, I said the lines under my breath.

Tom: "You came. I'm so glad."
Marilyn: "Rachmaninoff."
Tom: "The Second Piano Concerto."
Marilyn: "It isn't fair."
Tom: "Not fair? Why?"
Marilyn: "Every time I hear it I go to pieces."
Tom: "Oh?"
Marilyn: "May I sit next to you?"
Tom: "Please do."
Marilyn: "It shakes me and quakes me. It makes me feel goose pimply all over. I don't know where I am or who I am or what I'm doing. Don't stop. Don't stop. Don't ever stop."
Tom stops playing.
Marilyn: "Why did you stop?"
Tom: "You know why I stopped."
Marilyn: "Why?"
Tom: "Because—because now I'm going to take you in my arms and kiss you . . . very quickly and very hard. . . ."

That scene always slayed me. The three of us used to play it out in my bedroom over and over again, and we always fought over who could read Tom's lines. We always wanted to be Tom.

And then Marilyn—the real Marilyn—came into the room. I put down my drink and shot to my feet. She was wearing slacks, a large sweater, and sandals. No makeup. She looked absolutely, earthshakingly beautiful. She also looked puzzled. I guess she wondered why I was there instead of Roy but was too polite to say anything. I was absolutely tongue-tied and I'm not even sure I got out my name.

"I'm ready for a drive," she said, and I loved the way she said it. I wanted her to say it over and over again.

She took my arm, and I walked her to the car. I knew I must be dreaming, and the last thing I wanted to do was wake up.

As we drove along the Pacific Coast Highway I turned on the radio, low. "You Belong to Me" by the Duprees was playing.

"I like that," she said.

I nodded, too overcome by her presence to even speak. The silence could have been heavy, but it wasn't. It was a comfortable silence, at least at first, where you didn't feel you had to fill the empty spaces with a lot of static. Marilyn looked at the shoreline, her face turned away from me. There really wasn't much to see in the dark and all, but she kept on looking anyway. Her hair blew in the wind, she had one leg tucked up beneath the other, and her arms circled her body against the chill in the air. In fact it was cold enough to freeze the balls off a brass monkey. I wanted to offer her my jacket, but I was afraid to break the spell. She seemed so completely at peace as we drove along. I snuck a few looks at her, but I was afraid she'd catch me at it and mostly I kept my eyes on the road.

For about five minutes the silence was okay—nothing to write home about, but it didn't get on my nerves. When it went on, though, I started getting panicky. We weren't exactly off to a flying start. She was saying nothing, I was saying nothing; she just kept staring at the dark space where the ocean was. You could hear the waves lapping when they hit the shore. I began to get the feeling I'd kidnapped her. Finally she turned to me.

Okay, I thought. This is it. This is the beginning. She was going to talk to me, tell me something important. I was about to receive some wisdom, some sort of message that would straighten out my screwed-up self. I waited. Nothing. Not one single word. She sighed and turned back to her contemplation of the ocean. The silence was now deafening. I wasn't sure I could take much more of it. What was I going to report to Roy and Scott—that we just sat with each other for two hours like a couple of retards?

Right then I heard a police siren and saw flashing lights coming up behind me fast. The voice through the loudspeaker told me to pull over on the shoulder. I came to a careful stop and said a little prayer. I knew I wasn't speeding. It had to be a taillight or something. I wanted to tell Marilyn I could handle it, and even though I couldn't get a word out I sensed she understood. I quickly got out of the car and hurried over to the cop who was still sitting in the car writing something on a pad.

"Is there some problem, Officer? I know I wasn't speeding."

He slowly looked up at me like I was a bug that had just spattered on his windshield. "Did I ask you to get out of the car?"

"No. I—I just thought it would save you the trouble if I came back here and ex—"

"Stand back from the car."

"Yes, sir."

I nervously looked back at Marilyn, but she was staring out at the ocean again. It was like we weren't there.

"Take out your driver's license and registration," the cop said. I fumbled for my wallet and handed my license over, trembling like a spastic.

He studied it carefully and then gave me the cold blue-eyed stare those guys must study at the police academy. "Are you aware the car you're driving was reported stolen four days ago?"

"What? Oh, no, no—it wasn't *stolen*. I mean, he—my friend . . . I mean, I'm just borrowing it from a friend who . . . I mean, I borrowed it from him, and he borrowed it from his dad without—I guess without him knowing. His dad, I mean. Jesus, that does sound pretty bad."

We walked over to the Galaxie while I went on sputtering and stammering. I searched through the glove compartment for the registration, my fingers only inches from Marilyn's breasts.

"I can't find the registration. Please, sir, you have to believe me, this car isn't stolen; it's borrowed. I swear to you—I swear on my father's grave."

But suddenly he didn't seem all that interested in me or the car. His eyes were riveted on Marilyn, and he had a stupid grin on his face.

She smiled her most dazzling smile. "I'm sure this is Mr. Darpinian's car. I'm so bad with first names." She looked at me for help.

"Albert," I said promptly. "Roy's dad is Albert. He owns the car."

"As a matter of fact," said the cop, his eyes fastened to Marilyn's face like glue to paper, "that is the registered owner's name. Albert Darpinian."

"Roy's dad," I said.

"We *know* that," said the cop impatiently. Then, with a big grin for Marilyn, he said, "I'm sorry for the inconvenience, Miss Monroe. It's probably a mistake out of Dispatch. It happens. But you better tell your friend to get this car home pronto."

"Yes, sir," I said. "Thank you, sir." But he totally ignored me.

"Ma'am," he said, "could I trouble you for your autograph? To Fred?" He handed Marilyn his book of tickets and a pen. She signed and returned them to him.

"Good night, ma'am," he said, touching his cap to his forehead like some moonstruck kid. "Happy motoring." With a final frown at me, he strolled back to his car and took off, burning rubber.

I turned to Marilyn and found the courage to look directly into her eyes while she was looking at me. "Thank you," I said. Those were the first words I managed to say to her.

In answer, she reached over and brushed the hair from my forehead. I thought I might die on the spot from an overdose of happiness.

I remembered the look she gave Tom Ewell in *The Seven Year Itch* when she came down the stairs to old Tom's apartment dressed in a nightgown, carrying a hammer and a cup with a toothbrush in it. "Hi," I remembered her saying. "I forgot about the stairs. Isn't that silly? It was so easy. I just pulled out the nails. You know what? We can do this all summer." Then she gave him this extremely sensual look that really put him away. She looked a little like that when she brushed the hair away from my forehead, and *I* was put away. The look wasn't exactly like the one she gave Tom, though. It was maybe more tender and even a little motherly or something.

We pulled the car off the road at Zuma Beach and walked along the shoreline, carrying our shoes. I don't know what it was that finally opened her up, but suddenly her chest cracked open and her heart came pouring out to me. She wasn't a fantasy. She was a rose without thorns. She was real, she was warm, she was different from my dreams, and better. A living, breathing human being who talked to me about kindnesses and love and failures and kids. She told me about the loss of her father and how much it had hurt. I realized her life, like mine, had become a series of endings. And that was when it hit me why we were brought together: she was the one person in the world who could understand what was going on inside me—understand that emptiness left by my father that had always been with me, driving me nuts.

We sat on a hill of dry sand back from the surf, and Marilyn picked up a smooth stone and caressed it as she went on talking. She had never known her own father. In her dreams he was always this faceless man standing in the shadows. It really delighted her when I told her about my father, the few moments I still remembered clearly. I found myself confessing to her how he wanted most for me to be a good man and how I felt I had failed him. She looked at me and blinked once, twice. For one awful moment I thought she was going to burst into tears.

She took my hand and said, "If your father was here, I know he'd be proud of the man you *are*. That's what I think."

I still don't know how she did it with those few simple words, but all the fear I'd been living with for so many years was suddenly gone. And somehow, without putting it into words, she made me see what being a good man really meant. Being a good man didn't mean being a better man in some abstract way. It meant living a full life and being happy. She beamed this smile at me—this warm, wide, spectacular smile. We held hands and looked into each other's eyes. At that moment I would have done anything for her. But all I could think was to reach down and pick up a few grains of sand. I offered them to her.

"I wish these were diamonds," I said.

"They're diamonds if you say they are."

Then I handed her Roy's shoes. "I want you to have these," I said. "Like a keepsake. They belong to Roy, and I know he'd want you to have them—you know, like to remember us by."

She squeezed my hand, and I remembered word for word, right then, this terrific moment in *The Seven Year Itch* when Marilyn says to Tom, "But there's another guy in the room. Way over in the corner. Maybe he's kind of nervous and shy and perspiring a little. First, he looks past you. But then you sort of sense that he's gentle and kind and worried, that he'll be tender with you, and nice and sweet. That's what's really exciting. If I were your wife I'd be very jealous of you. I'd be very, very jealous. I think you're just elegant." I'd always fantasized that Marilyn was saying those words to me, not Tom, and now in a funny way I really believe she *had* been saying them to me all along.

On the drive back to her house we got really silent again. But this time the silence wasn't threatening. I parked at the end of the driveway and ran around and opened the door for Marilyn. I held a hand out to help her. She took a firm grip of both my hands and slowly kissed them. I felt a shock, sort of like a burning—but a beautiful burning. It coursed right through my body to the bone. She then took me in her arms and held me close, and I'd never felt as safe and as warm in anyone's arms before. Her lips gently brushed my cheek and then, tenderly and only for a second, but a second that would last forever, her lips touched mine.

"Thanks for the drive, Ned."

She gave my face a final caress, then walked up the drive to the front door. I watched her walk away, knowing that for the rest of my life I would see her walking away from me. I would be watching that little hip wiggle of hers, not exaggerated like in the movies, and knowing it would always be with me. After she waved and then disappeared inside the house, I went on standing there in the darkness that was beginning to lighten just a shade toward dawn. I brought my hands up to my nose and inhaled deeply. Marilyn was still there, on my fingers. As I smiled, remembering her touch and the electric charge it gave me, I thought about never washing my hands again.

Sixteen

When I got back to Harvey's, Roy and Scott were waiting up for me in the bomb shelter, even though by then it was almost morning.

"Hi, guys," I said with a huge grin.

"Bleuer, you son of a bitch," said Roy. "I just know you paddled the old canoe."

I shook my head. "That's *your* fantasy, Roy."

"You mean you didn't?" Scott said, looking relieved. "So what happened? Fill us in. Spare us nothing."

"It was incredible. She's the most incredible woman—not at all like her movies. She said she was flattered we found her so attractive. But she wanted us to know her for herself."

"Sure, they all say that," said Roy. "But what about the canoe trip? Don't bullshit me now."

"I told you, Roy, that just wasn't in the picture. I hate to disappoint you, but—"

"Oh, Christ, you mooch my date and then you don't even canoe her? You don't even give it the old college try? Dood coulda done that."

I shook my head. "None of us would've done it."

"I woulda, you better believe it. She ain't the Virgin Mary, the last I heard. If I'm gonna go out with her. I'm gonna leave her something to remember me by."

"Don't worry. She'll remember you. I gave her your shoes."

They both looked down and saw I was standing there in my stocking feet.

"Okay," Roy said. "You put 'em to good use."

While I went on answering questions—they fired them at me like it was a presidential press conference and I was the president—we stormed the kitchen and cooked up a big predawn for-the-road breakfast. I fried a pound of bacon while Scott made pancake batter. Roy sat watching us work—as usual. Our plan was to eat and then hit the road early, heading for Indian Springs.

"Hey, Dood, you really think Bleuer went over to Marilyn's house? Or did he run the car down the street and polish his woody?"

"Of course he went."

"Of course I went."

"Can you prove it?"

"I don't have to prove it."

"He doesn't have to prove it," said Scott.

"What are you guys, an echo chamber?" Roy lit a cigarette and blew out a big sickening cloud of smoke. I forced this big cough just to let him know I didn't like it.

"How can you light up before breakfast?" Scott said.

"Easy. You take a cigarette out of the pack and put a match to it. Or in my case a Zippo lighter."

"But aren't they disgusting on an empty stomach?"

"A cigarette's a cigarette. They always taste good." To show us how much he liked smoking, old Roy drew in a big drag and inhaled it through his nose, French style. "You know this funny feeling I've got?"

We looked at him.

"What is it, Roy?" Scott said.

"Probably indigestion," I said.

"It's like we've been climbing a mountain for years, one where you can't get to the top. The Marilyn mountain. And we finally reach the top. Wow—we made it! That's the way we feel, but we also feel kinda empty. At least I do. Because once you've got there, where do you go from there?"

"That's deep, Roy," I said, holding the spatula in the air and staring at him. "I know what you mean. I kind of feel that way myself."

"Me too," said Scott.

"It's like I've gotta do something else now," Roy said. "My life's gotta turn a corner."

"You're gonna be a soldier boy," said Scott. "I'd say that's turning a corner."

"Hey, Dood," said Roy, "I've been thinkin' about that Howdy Doody contest way back when we were little kids. If you'd had to pick one person to be Howdy Doody's special friend who would it've been—me or Ned?"

"Why are you asking me this?"

"Yeah, why are you asking him?" I said.

"Shut up, echo chamber," Roy said. "Come on, Dood. Just give me an answer."

"I probably would've picked Becky to be my special Howdy Doody friend."

"Becky?"

"I couldn't ever choose between you two guys. You're both my best friends. How could I hurt one of you by choosing the other?"

"You're so soft, Dood. I always figured Bleuer here was the only reason you hung around with me."

"What a paranoid," I said.

"You're all wrong," Scott said to Roy. "The thing about you is, you never let me off the hook. Never. I always end up doing what you want me to do, even if I feel guilty or half nuts doing it."

"Me too," I said.

"So what you're both sayin' is, you don't like me because I get you drunk; you like me because I hang around while you throw up and then I toss you a towel."

"Something like that," said Scott.

Roy dropped his cigarette in the remains of the batter.

"Jesus, Roy, how gross can you get?" I said.

"You know what woulda made my trip, Dood?" said Roy, ignoring my comment. "I shoulda got you canoed."

Scott looked at him and then at me, cleared his throat nervously, and said, "Have you ever considered the possibility—you know, that Becky and I have done everything already?"

Roy waved his arm like he was swatting a fly. "What are you, outta your mind?"

"Impossible," I said.

"Why impossible?" Scott said.

"'Cause you're the Dood," said Roy. "You listen to other people talk about it."

"You know what I really think?" said Scott. "I think all the guys like you who talk about it so much aren't getting any. It's the guys like me who never talk about it who get it all the time."

I laughed. "Don't flatter yourself, Dood."

"You're bein' a pea-brain," Roy said.

"Okay, you guys," Scott said with a mysterious smile, and dropped the subject.

* * *

When Roy and I were packed and ready to go, we said good-bye to Harvey and thanked him for everything. He was so impressed with my date with Marilyn and everything, he gave me the jacket I'd worn and told me never to get it dry-cleaned. We rushed out to the Galaxie and piled into the back. A few minutes later Scott came limping out, and when he saw us sitting back there he stopped, dropped his clothing bag on the ground, and stared at us. Roy had left the driver's door open, the key in the ignition, and the engine running.

"What's the idea?" said Scott.

"You're the big idea," I said.

"Remember in the kitchen you told me I never let you off the hook?" Roy said. "Well, I ain't about to start now. Home, Dood."

Scott walked kind of gingerly around the car like it was a wild animal about to mow him down. He stopped at the open door. "I can't do it."

"We're sick of your sayin' 'I can't' all the time," Roy said. "In fact we're gonna rule 'I can't' out of your vocabulary. From now on when you don't wanna do something your new word is 'I'mapussy' —one word that says all. You got it?"

"What if I get in an accident?"

"What if I get pregnant?"

"Seriously."

"It won't matter. You don't have a license, you don't have insurance, and you're driving a stolen car. An accident's minor."

"Think positive, Dood," I said.

He climbed in behind the wheel. Right then Harvey came outside in his silk bathrobe for a final good-bye but, without warning, Scott hit the gas pedal, sending the Galaxie roaring down the driveway and leaving old Harvey in a cloud of dust.

Roy and I hung our heads out the window.

"Good-bye, Harvey!"

"Take 'er easy, Unc!"

Scott hunched forward, gripping the wheel so hard his knuckles turned white, his hands at the correct ten-o'clock and two-o'clock position. Knowing Scott, he'd probably already read the driver's manual—he read everything he could get his hands on. The thing that impressed Roy and me was how fast he drove. He ran the Galaxie like he was late for an accident. On one flat stretch of desert highway I leaned over the front seat to check the speedometer—125 miles an hour! It seemed like we got home in about ten minutes, and by the time we pulled up in front of Scott's house he was jabbering about getting a driver's license. Somehow I knew he wasn't going to go through the rest of his life between the quotation marks.

He seemed sad that the trip was over. He got out of the car and said to Roy, "Am I gonna see you before you go?"

"Feast your eyes on me now 'cause I'm vapor."

"No, you'll see the Dood tomorrow," I told him. "We'll all meet at the train station."

"Yeah, the train station," said Roy as he removed his sunglasses and climbed behind the wheel.

"I'm glad we did this, Roy," Scott said. "Thanks for getting me out of town. See you guys at the station."

"One o'clock," I said. "Don't be late, Dood."

"Hose yourself off before you get there, Darpinian," said Scott. "You smell like a cow."

"Like Evelyn," I said.

"You guys should talk," said Roy. "You know what they say: a skunk smells his own hole first."

Scott picked up his bag. "God, I feel like I got about six years of explaining to do."

"You know," I said, "I haven't told you guys this: Marilyn's not perfect."

Scott looked shocked. "She's not?"

"She's pudgier than we thought. Shorter, too. And she's got a few wrinkles. She does have nice eyes, though. But so does Becky."

"Yeah, Becky does have great eyes." Scott grinned. "I guess I'm lucky to have her, right? I guess Marilyn's a little old for me." He swung his clothing bag up in the air in a wave and walked up the path to his house.

Roy wanted to drop me at home, but I insisted on going with him to return the car. If his old man got really hot I wanted to be there to take my share of the blame.

Mr. Darpinian was alone in the gym working out at the punching bag. Roy tossed the car keys across the room; they landed at his father's feet. Roy picked up a pair of boxing gloves and walked toward his father. I leaned against the wall, trying to make myself invisible.

"I brought your car back," Roy said. "There's fifty or seventy-five bucks' worth of damage to the right fender. I'll pay for it."

"From the money you stole."

"That's my business. I'll take care of it."

"You also stole my car. You had no right takin' it."

"I borrowed it."

"I figured you for gone already."

"It's Saturday." Roy started to remove his shirt. "I got some ring time comin'."

"Since when?"

"You owe me."

"You step in the ring there are no more lessons, Roy. This time it's gonna be for real."

"I know," said Roy as he put on his gloves. "That's the way I want it."

He motioned to me, and I went up and laced his gloves for him. "Hello, Mr. Darpinian."

"Ned."

"Sorry about the car."

"It's not your fault."

"I was part of it," I said and then retreated to the wall again. I wanted to disappear down a black hole. The feeling I had was that I was about to see something I shouldn't be seeing.

They circled around, kind of feeling each other out at first. Suddenly Roy attacked his father with a furious volley of blows. Then, with a wild right hook, he knocked Mr. Darpinian right on his ass on the canvas.

"I . . . love . . . you," Roy whispered.

I could barely hear him, and I could hardly believe what I was hearing, but that was what he said.

On his hands and knees, his father said, "What did you say?"

"Nothin'. Come on, let's get it on."

They started trading blows, but it was clear that Mr. Darpinian was no longer a match for his son. Roy slammed his father against the ropes with a hard straight right to the jaw. As Mr. Darpinian slumped to a sitting position, Roy whispered again, "I . . . love . . . you."

"What the hell are you sayin'?" Mr. Darpinian glared at Roy as he wiped blood from his nose with his glove.

"I ain't sayin' nothin'. What would I be sayin'? Get up."

Roy held out his gloves to help his father up.

That's when Mr. Darpinian really got into it. He must have realized he couldn't hold back, that he had to give it everything he had. Roy and his old man stood toe to toe pounding each other. It was gruesome to watch and yet kind of exciting, too, in a morbid sort of way. Roy, who was smaller than his father, seemed to be running out of steam; he clinched to get his breath. Mr. Darpinian tried to break the hold, but Roy wouldn't let him move away. They staggered around the ring that way, like two drunks dancing. And then I began to realize that Roy was actually hugging his old man and Mr. Darpinian was returning the embrace. Finally they moved apart and stared at each other. I could see tears in Roy's eyes.

"What's gotten into you?" his father said.

"I'm not gonna be around for a while. I figured, what the hell. My last few minutes can be with you."

"Wipe the sweat from your eyes."

Roy used his gloves to wipe away his tears. "You had enough?" he asked.

"If you have," said Mr. Darpinian.

Roy slung a glove around his father's shoulders and Mr. Darpinian gave Roy a playful cuff on the top of his head. As they hugged each other I could see Roy's shoulders shaking. It was too much for me, and I beat it out of there.

* * *

The next afternoon we all met at the railroad station. I guess Scott needed Roy and me there for support while he tried to square things with Becky.

He held her hand and said, "Becky, when we get married I want us to start out right. Nothing hidden, nothing standing between us. And I'm—Well, I've lied to you already. . . ." He looked over at us for help, but he was on his own; it was his situation and he had to work it out his way. "I've got this thing I have to clear up."

Becky grinned up at him. "Is this about Marilyn?"

"Yeah. But how did you know that?"

"It was obvious you guys were gonna do this. I mean you'd been talking about it for years, and to tell the truth I'm glad you decided to go. You had to get it out of your system."

Scott shook his head. "But it's more than that. I didn't just go to see her—you know, meet her and get her autograph or something. I wanted to marry her."

"Christ, Dood," Roy said.

"Shut up," I said to Roy.

Becky stared at Scott and then started laughing. "Sweetheart, you never would've married her. Not in a million years."

Scott looked indignant. "I was planning on it."

"You never would've done it. You really wouldn't. I know you too well." She touched Scott's cheek. "You love *me*."

"She's right, Dood," said Roy. "You wouldn't last a day without old Beck here."

She turned to Roy, smiled, and gave him a playful punch in the gut. She studied his puffy eyes and cut lip. "Whose lawnmower ran over you?"

"I did a little boxing with my old man."

"He boxed, you ducked. But you didn't duck enough."

"I guess so."

The wedding's not gonna be the same without you, Roy Darpinian."

"Maybe I can get a leave."

"You'd better," said Scott.

"Or I can go AWOL. Your wedding's a good cause. Like a family emergency."

"No way," said Scott. "You're not gonna screw up this military thing."

"You know," Roy said to Becky, "all your kids are gonna look like him. Are you prepared for that?"

Becky hugged Roy and kissed him on the lips. "We're gonna miss you, stupid."

The train whistle blew.

"Hey, you guys," she said, quickly grabbing her Polaroid from her purse. "I gotta get your tattoos on film."

"How do you know about the tattoos?" I said.

"Scott showed me his. He told me about yours. Come on, boys, give me some flesh."

So we rolled up our pants and Becky shot Scott's

wooden—his right—leg, my right leg, and Roy's right leg, three tattoos of a heart cracked open with Marilyn's face emerging from the center.

Then Roy shook hands with Scott and me. I guess it was the only time we'd ever shaken hands in all the years we'd known one another.

"Whatever you do, don't die," Scott said.

"Shit, that's the last thing I'm gonna do."

The train whistle blew again.

I walked up to Roy and opened my Marilyn Bible. Stuck inside was the picture of Marilyn she had autographed and mailed to the three of us six years ago. It was pretty yellowed now, and water stained, too, from the swim it took in the Pacific Ocean when the Gallo brothers were hot after us. I removed it and handed it to Roy. He took it, stared at it and then looked at his feet. I could tell he was embarrassed—his neck turned kind of red.

"Remember how we all fought over who should keep it?"

"Yeah, I remember," Roy said. "Three little snot-nosed twelve-year-olds."

"Speak for yourself," said Scott, grinning.

I looked at Scott and gave a little nod; he nodded in return.

"I want you to have this, too, Roy," I said, and handed him the Bible. "I think you deserve it the most."

He held the Bible gingerly, like a father holding a newborn baby. "Why?" he said. "Why me?"

"You got us out there to L.A. You made it all happen. If it hadn't been for you, Marilyn would have always been a dream."

"You were a big learning experience," Scott said, punching Roy on the arm. "And those few days were like a year of college. I don't know what I'd be like if we hadn't gone to find her."

Roy looked at us both and said, "Well, thanks. Thanks, good buddies. You know she's in good hands with me."

I grabbed Roy and gave him this huge bear hug.

"I'm gonna miss you, Darpinian," I said. "About this much . . ." I showed him about an inch of space between my thumb and index finger.

Roy laughed and quickly pulled away from me. I guess he was a little embarrassed. He gave Becky a peck on the cheek and walked over to Mr. Darpinian, who'd just arrived and was standing a ways down the platform. They spoke for a moment, and they actually looked pretty happy together, like a father and son who really liked each other. Then Roy jumped up the steps onto the train. We all waved furiously as the train pulled out of the station, but we never got a glimpse of him.

So another ending in my life happened that day, but not a bad one. I had a good feeling about Roy—that no matter what, there would always be a Roy Darpinian running around loose somewhere in the world.

Seventeen

When college started in late August, I found myself not at Harvard but back in California on the UCLA campus. It seemed like years since I was out there with Roy and Scott, although it was only a couple of months. Our pilgrimage to Marilyn was like part of another life—and now Marilyn was dead. It was still hard for me to accept her death. I would never forget the day I got the news of her passing. It was hot as a pistol. I was working in the toy store, demonstrating a spinning top for this lady and her brood of little brats and Johnny Tillotson was singing "Send Me the Pillow That You Dream On" on the radio. That moment is engraved on my memory forever. When the song ended, an announcer came on and said, "One of the most famous stars in Hollywood is dead at thirty-six. Marilyn Monroe was found dead this morning. . . ." The rest I don't remember. My brain shut down. I just walked out of the store and went home.

I took off my jacket, the jacket I had worn that night with Marilyn, and some sand fell out of the pocket. The whole universe had suddenly stopped. We were one gigantic broken heart.

So much of my life I don't have explanations for. I still don't understand how Scott can look like Howdy Doody and have a wooden leg. Or my father being called a hero because he was the wrong person in the wrong place at the wrong time. Or Marilyn . . . She was loved by so many people. How could she die all alone on a Saturday night? Maybe death is that part of life we're not meant to understand. Maybe life isn't for everyone. Or maybe loving someone with all our heart is just the great chance we take.

By the time I was scheduled to report to college, I was relieved to be getting out of Indian Springs, and frankly I think Mom was just as glad to get rid of me for a while. The last thing I did before boarding the bus for Los Angeles was to lock my dad's watch—still giving the same old time: two-oh-nine—in his old rolltop desk and retrieve my Timex. It was still ticking.

My second day at college I was struggling across

campus trying to balance a stack of textbooks and study a campus map at the same time. I was late for a chemistry class and didn't have the slightest idea where to go. Ahead of me a small crowd was gathering. I figured maybe one of the kids could help me, so I walked up to them, and then I saw this girl standing in the rear of the pack. It was like a bolt of lightning—the same bolt that had struck me six years earlier when I found Dad's old "Golden Dreams" calendar and my love affair with Marilyn began.

I could only see the girl from behind, but her hair, her clothes, her stance, her size—they were all Marilyn. It was like I was in some kind of dream, the kind you never want to end. I moved as close to her as I could, and then I saw what the crowd was up to. Students were stuffing themselves inside a phone booth. There were maybe half a dozen inside so far and more were piling in. It seemed kind of insane.

I finally got up my nerve and tapped the girl on the shoulder. When she turned to me, my heart sank. She was a pretty girl, but she was no Marilyn. She wasn't even remotely like Marilyn, except for her blond hair, and even though I'd known that she couldn't be Marilyn, I found it hard not to show my disappointment.

"Can you tell me what's going on here?" I asked.
"We're trying to break the record from last year."
"Really? How many people?"

"Twenty-five."

"You got to be kidding. Twenty-five?"

Just as I found myself feeling kind of attracted to the girl, even if she wasn't any Marilyn, she suddenly ran off and joined the people already crammed in the booth. I guess it took me about one second to come to a decision. I dropped my books to the ground and squeezed into the phone booth tight against her.

"How many so far?"

"I think you make twelve."

"And the record's twenty-five?"

"Yep, and we need twenty-six. It's gonna be tough."

Another student wedged himself into the booth forcing this increasingly pretty girl inches closer to me.

"I'm Ned Bleuer," I said. "A freshman."

"Melissa Smock. Sophomore."

She gave me this absolutely magnificent smile.

Okay, so she had this horrible last name. Okay, so she wasn't Marilyn. I wasn't my father, either. We were just two people trying to make a little mark on the world right now by getting twenty-six people into a phone booth. And if we failed at this or anything we tried, we failed. Who cared? In the long run all you can really do is go forward.

Right then the telephone rang in the booth. We all did a kind of bump and grind so somebody could answer the phone. In the process, Melissa and I were forced right up against each other. Well, why not take the next step? I told myself. So I kissed her for the first time. I figured Roy was right when he said you can't rub Ben-Gay on a heartache.